# MOUNTAIN RAT

## by George Erdstein

PublishAmerica
Baltimore

ISBN: 1-4241-8219-0
PUBLISHED BY PUBLISHAMERICA, LLLP
www.publishamerica.com
Baltimore

Printed in the United States of America

# MOUNTAIN RAT

# PROLOGUE

It seemed as if the summer had only begun when my family and I headed up north in late August. Yet, returning to Detroit from Glen Arbor only two weeks later, the trees were already starting to change color. I rolled down the window to allow the scent of the aging season to waft through the van. Holding the wheel and seeing my suntanned forearms, I smiled, anticipating admiring comments from my nursing staff the next day. The vacation had been a good one, with only one day of rain and no emergency calls from the office. I had played some decent tennis and even got to the finals in the Mixed-Doubles tournament. Glancing at my partner sitting next to me, I saw her fast asleep, her creased eyes and Mona Lisa smile hinting at a contented dream within.

Suspicious of the uncommon quiet in the rear, I risked a backward glimpse to see, among the mounds of luggage, two deeply breathing lumps resembling my offspring. All is at peace, I thought, and fumbled for a classical tape befitting the mood of the moment. "Perfect," I said aloud, and let Beethoven's Sixth Symphony slide into the tape deck.

On either side of the great Michigan concrete highway, endless rows of majestic pines whizzed by, spelled only by a subtle patchwork of orange and yellow puffs. And above, an occasional cloud dotted the aqua sky, seeming to reflect the only occasional appearance of another car on the road.

I was cruising at 65, only 10 miles over the new speed limit, and feeling very mellow, conducting the "Pastorale" with my free forefinger. A late model Cadillac inched up in the left lane, kept pace for about half a mile, then moved forward. Just below its 1980 license plate, a bumper sticker appeared and in bold blue on white letters read, "DO IT IN THE CATSKILLS." I stopped conducting and stared at the inscription, my breath temporarily on hold. The Cadillac moved on and then disappeared.

"DO IT IN THE CATSKILLS," I mused, and pensively mouthed the words to myself again…. and again.

# CHAPTER 1

It was there all right. Fading in with the landlady-green wall the sign read, "Prestige Employment Agency—One Flight Up." This was not quite the introduction I expected, having heard that this was *the* place to get summer work. Nor had I dragged myself downtown that afternoon in unseasonably hot weather because I enjoyed wallowing in the honky-tonk of Times Square. The boys at Tau Alpha Pi warned me if I wanted to find work in the mountains at all that summer, I had better get my ass down to Prestige—pronto. I resented having to leave my books just two weeks before finals, even for an afternoon, just to line up a job I had heard compared to slave labor. True, some of the guys had wild stories to tell, and others talked of making four times the money one could expect playing it safe as a camp counselor. So here I was. "But what's the rush," I thought, opening the partially painted glass door to the stairway.

As I ascended, the unmistakable stench of sweating male bodies descended on me. At the top of the stairs I was greeted by a thick layer of cigarette smoke, which, with the gorilla odor or "G.O.," as the neighborhood boys dubbed it, brought me almost to the point of nausea. A large hand-printed sign was taped to the wall—"1957 SUMMER JOBS ONLY." Looking about the tall Spartan space surrounded on three sides by half-high obscured-glass cubicles, I was confronted with a bedraggled army of bored-looking aspiring mountain rats. Some, seated on multi-initialed folding wooden chairs, were either staring at the repetitively patterned metal stamped ceiling or glaring at a half-smoked cigarette dangling limply from a knee-supported hand. Others, half-standing against the one full wall in the room, were mumbling in small groups and belching an occasional raw giggle.

I worked my way to the focal point of the assemblage—a linoleum-topped green metal desk which might have served an army recruiting station—for both wars. There, typing file cards non-stop, sat a middle-aged biddy with thick seashell-framed glasses.

"Excuse me, ma'am," I offered. She glanced up. "I'd like to inquire about summer work as a busboy or waiter…."

She stopped, slipped a blank card into the carriage and groaned, "You'll have to see Mr. Sharman. Give me your name and address."

"Phillip Dechter—245 Pinehurst Avenue, New York 33."

"Got a phone?"

"Yeah, sure. Wadsworth 3-8572."

The typewriter gunned the information onto the card, then the seashells looked up blankly, "Have a seat. Mr. Sharman will be with you shawtly." I looked around, found no empty seat, so ambled over to the nearest stretch of unoccupied wall where I could lean and wait and observe.

"Greaseballs, all greaseballs," I thought to myself. Could I compete with them? Could I work with them? My hands were wet. Twenty minutes passed. My eyes met another pair equally doubtful and I wondered, "Maybe we're all the same—what the heck."

"Berkowitz!" barked a short fat cigar emerging from a cubicle and immediately dominated the room.

"That's Sharman," offered a nearby leaning voice.

"Oh, yeah?" I glanced over obligingly. "Is he as rough as he sounds?"

"Yeah! He'll scare the shit out of you, but if there's a job out there he'll get it for you." I saw in my informer a darkly skinny, wanting-to-be-liked homely type, no doubt from Brooklyn. Together we watched the summoned Berkowitz being hurriedly led into the cubicle by Mr. Sharman. "He's a dummy."

"Who's a dummy?"

"Berkowitz," retorted Brooklyn. "He's wearing pegged pants. Sharman don't like pegged pants. He wants to know you've been around but he don't like greaseballs...... See this shirt?"

I looked carefully at Brooklyn's sweat-stained seersucker shirt. "Yeah, I see it. What about it?"

"It's the uniform. Everybody in the mountains wears a white seersucker shirt—that is, if you're smart. You can wash it every night, let it dry, and it won't be wrinkled in the morning. Sharman likes to see you know your way around. Know what I mean?"

"You sound like you've been around," I said sarcastically.

"Yeah. I worked a couple of years in Fleischmanns, but this year I'm gonna work the other side of the mountains. Say, I'm Marv Dickstein," he said, extending his hand. Given little choice, I shook hands and nodded obligingly, but said nothing as my eyes darted about in search of escape.

"Dickstein!" growled the barker.

"That's me!" he jumped. "Maybe I'll see you up in the mountains, huh?" Marv Dickstein retreated, then trotted off in the direction of the awaiting Mr. Sharman.

I was alone now. "Shit," I thought, "the guy wasn't really that bad. Why didn't I introduce myself? I did it again. The guy was starting to give me useful information. What is the other side of the mountains? I'll bet I'm the only jerk in the room who doesn't know about seersucker shirts." What else didn't I know that I should? I looked around. The crowd seemed to be thinning out. A radio in a nearby office was playing the Platters' "Only You." My thoughts drifted to the past Saturday night when I was listening to the same tune while making out with Carol—not stuck in this awful place. She had such a nice smell, comfortable like a newborn baby. But her body definitely belonged to Mother Earth. Big, rounded parts with smooth delicious folds, but not fat. There were no angles to her body at all. Even her hair, cut in a page-boy, arched forward, making her face appear rounder than it actually was. Mom would like Carol because she was zaftig. My mother didn't trust girls who were too bony.

A door slammed, rattling the structure of the cubicle surrounding it. The stale scent of spent cigarettes still hung in the air. I thought maybe I could still duck out before being summoned. This whole business wasn't for me.

"Dechter!"

I slowly approached Sharman, struck by the feeling that all the stench and tension in the room emanated from that one cigar. The whole cubicle shook again as the door slammed behind me and Sharman dropped into his well-worn, early rustic, swivel-tilt chair.

"Sit down, kid! Hot out there, huh? Where'd you work before?" he said non-stop, interested only in the answer to the last question.

Taken aback by this quick pace and distracted by Sharman's ridiculous yellow toupee, I blurted out, "I've never worked in a hotel...but I spent two summers as a camper-waiter...and of course I've had some part-time jobs in the city, one in a drugstore as..."

"Nah, nah, nah!" Sharman interrupted. "Forget the drugstore. Can you hold a tray full of dirty dishes and race through Grand Central Station on Labor Day?"

Trying to picture the scene and respond at the same time, I chuckled weakly, "I guess I'd have to try it to know for sure."

Sharman's eyes started to roll. "You a college boy?"

"Yeah!"

"Where?"

"Columbia. I'm finishing my first year."

"They don't teach you how to make money, do they?" the cigar asked impatiently.

"Not directly. They prepare you to...."

"Bullshit! Let me tell you something, college—sonny boy. If you want to get ahead in this world, you don't say you gotta try it first before you know if you can do it. You say, 'Sure', and figure it out later. And you damn well better figure it out later. And that doesn't go for just pushing trays neither. You're a good lookin' kid, but you gotta have instinct. Anyhow, I don't have all day. I'll tell you what I'll do. I got a job here for a busboy at the Crystal Arms Hotel in Paradise Lake. Ever hear of it? It ain't Grossinger's but you can learn the ropes there, and if you play it right, you can make as much money as in the big houses. You want it?"

Hesitation. "Sounds real good. Can I ask you how much they pay?"

Eyes rolling, "Peanuts! You get bed, board and $15 a week. The rest is tips. If you're on your toes, you come home Labor Day with over a thousand bucks in your pocket. It's all up to you. You want it?"

"I'll take it," I said, totally cornered.

"Good. You'll go up over Memorial Day week-end for a trial run. If you work out, fine. If not, you're out. There are no guarantees in this business. A lot of kids come in here and give me a song and dance about having to work their way through college. Why? I don't know. Personally, I think it's a waste of time. Anyway, they go up to the mountains and expect everything to come to them on a silver platter. It don't work that way. You wanna work your way through college—then you gotta know what work is. There ain't no way you can make the bucks you make in the mountains—legally, that is, but you gotta work. Okay, kid? Give this slip to the girl outside. She'll give you the details." With that, he bombed out of the cubicle, leaving me in a cloud of Tampa's worst. Frantically, I pulled out my final exam schedule from my back pocket. Sure enough, the Tuesday after Memorial Day was my C.C. exam.

The subway ride home seemed endless. I was depressed. I knew the moment Sharman spoke of working the Memorial Day week-end I had a conflict. I also knew that if I had mentioned it, the whole job would have blown up in my face. So here I was, committed to giving my all to a job I had mixed emotions over, at a place I never heard of, and at a time I needed to be spending studying for my last exam, the toughest of them all—Contemporary Civilization. I gazed through the darkened subway window, watching my image jostle rhythmically with the motion of the car. The upturned collar of my windbreaker sliced through my wavy brown hair. My taller than average six foot frame and broad shoulders had always given me confidence. Now I tried to see myself as Sharman saw me. A good-looking kid? Yeah, I knew I was better looking than most. But what was this instinct stuff? Was I too careful and not gutsy enough? I looked closer at my reflection. My even features told me nothing. If I really wanted this job I should be feeling happy right now, looking forward not only to the challenge, but the adventure of it all. But how was I going to make up that lost study time? What did Sharman know about school anyhow? Surely he never got past Junior High. Grades were so important. One bomb on a final exam could spoil my chances of getting into medical school. Should I take the chance? My reflection shrugged back at me.... "Maybe I'll discuss it with my mother," I thought.

# CHAPTER 2

What a glorious morning—the Friday before a holiday week-end and not a cloud in sight. The Port Authority Bus Terminal, however, was another scene altogether. Slowly maneuvering busses belched volumes of black exhaust while promising to take the shoving, pushing crowds away from it all. Confused people with screaming children raced from gate to gate, while frailer folks wearing sunglasses stood by, nervously anticipating the year's first blush of fresh Catskill air.

I finally found the bus marked "Paradise Lake." On boarding, I was surprised to find a great number of elderly people, all seemingly oblivious to the chaos outside. Finding an empty pair of seats, I perched myself smugly against the window. I sighed with relief. I had done my part. The next step was the driver's, so why not relax and watch the rest of the crazy world go by. What a weird array of people. A redhead wearing tight toreador pants and high heels strutted by. Wow! "How come I'm so sure she's not going to the Crystal Arms Hotel?" I wondered. "This better not be an old age home. There's got to be some kind of action up there." My thoughts were interrupted by the presence of another body sitting beside me. It was a guy about nineteen or twenty. I hoped he was doing the same thing I was. We said nothing. The driver soon appeared and began counting heads as he casually worked his way down the aisle. When the bus was filled to his satisfaction, he closed the doors, set his reflective sunglasses in position and revved up the engine for the promised land.

As the bus emerged from the Lincoln Tunnel on New Jersey soil, the beauty of the day once again became evident. I felt a sense of deliverance from the oppression of the city. Memorial Day week-end was the first harbinger of summer, and as such, held much hope for all celebrants. I glanced again at my neighbor and inquired as casually as I could, "You going all the way to Paradise Lake?"

Two very dark but friendly eyes turned to me. "Yeah, I'm gonna work one of the hotels up there. How about you?"

"Same here. I'm going to be a busboy at the Crystal Arms."

"No kidding! That's where I'm going. But no kitchen for me. No man! That's too much of a rat race. I like the bellhop scene, myself. You're pretty much on your own and you get first crack at the chicks as they come in. This'll be my third year up there, you know," dark eyes offered eagerly, the peach fuzz under his large nose becoming a focal point for my attention.

"Really!" I was thrilled. "Tell me about the place. By the way, I'm Phil." I didn't want to make the same mistake again in this venture.

"Hi, I'm Mickey." We shook hands awkwardly. "Well, it's not the fanciest place around. In fact, some guys call it a schlock house. But that's okay with me. The Millers—they're the owners, are pretty nice as far as owners go. Some hotel owners are real bastards. They treat the help like real shit." He lowered his voice to a whisper and drew close to me. "You see the people on this bus? Most of them are refugees, the kind of people who come to the Arms. They feel comfortable up there. They come year after year and meet the same people all the time. They walk along the road and talk German. They've had it rough. So now they've got their own world up there." This had a familiar ring to me. I wondered why my parents had never told me about these resorts for refugees. Surely they would know about them. They were refugees themselves. True, they had gotten out of Europe before the war actually broke out, but they got out because they had to. They ran. Pop rarely talked about it. Mom never did. It seemed as if they wanted to disassociate themselves from the whole bloody Holocaust. It was a bad dream that never happened. Sometimes they acted as if they were not European Jews, but their accents betrayed them. They knew many other people from Vienna, but the friends they sought out were usually American-born.

Mickey continued, "Where does that leave us? I'll tell you one thing. If we were on the other side of the mountains there'd be more action 'cause there's more young stuff over there. But I'll also tell you this," his eyes smiling very confidently. "There's enough to go around right around 'ye olde hotel'." We both chuckled.

"Where does it come from?" I asked.

"First of all, you always have a few girls working at the hotel—behind the front desk or in the day camp. Then there are the occasional young guests, usually the daughters, who are as hungry as you are. Then there's the town. Paradise Lake is a great little town. But it's not like South Fallsburg. It sort of picks up the flavor of the refugees—kind of like a European mountain village—whatever that is." I listened intently, but could not keep my eyes off the peach fuzz decorating Mickey's upper lip. I wondered why he didn't shave and get it over with. "Anyhow," Mickey continued, "there are a lot of other hotels around—a couple larger, but most smaller than the Arms. And, oh yeah," his eyes lit up as he remembered, "there's a camp outside of town with great looking girls. But," Mickey added slowly, "they stick pretty much to themselves. They're really snobby bitches."

I detected bitterness in my companion's voice, something I could only attribute to the sad ending of a prior summer's romance. But I was interested and so pursued, "How's that, Mickey?"

Mickey rolled his eyes uneasily and then looked at me very deliberately. "They think they're better than we are. They think we're a grubby bunch, not like the casual Joe College counselor types." I wasn't quite ready to be lumped into Mickey's "we" group. I hadn't as yet lifted a tray or even seen the hotel for that matter. Besides, I liked to think of myself as a Joe College—casual, definitely not grubby. Not yet a mountain rat, I was already denying the baggage. As I think back, I was forever looking for an escape valve, an option to shift gears should the situation prove uncomfortable. I looked out the window. Maybe I was jumping to conclusions. Maybe this kid sitting next to me was all wet, had an inferiority complex or something. He sure as hell didn't look like an ass-man—too short and wiry, sort of a jockey type. I could handle those camp girls, I assured myself.

The bright sky was interrupted as the bus turned into a canyon carved through the Catskill foothills. I saw my reflection in the darkened window and instinctively protruded my chin, a habit I had developed but wasn't sure why.

"Anyhow," Mickey interrupted my drifting, "the town's got a few jumping places where everybody goes and you get to know who works where pretty soon. You know, you guys have it better than me in one respect. You work your asses off all day, but when you're done cleaning up after dinner, you're free. I've got it easier, but I'm on almost all goddamn day and night. If it's not picking up an old biddy at the bus station, it's running a poker game in the card room."

"Hey, wait a minute," I laughed. "I haven't started this job yet. I don't know if I'm going to last past this week-end. Let's not worry about who's got it better just yet, okay?"

"Okay," Mickey shrugged defensively.

Someone, two seats in front of us, opened a window, allowing the scent of wild chives to penetrate the bus. I drank it in, in silent euphoria. That, to me, was the essence of spring. Smells had always meant something special. They had the ability of conjuring up a memory—exactly, not like a photograph which is viewed with ever-increasing perspective—and tainted by time. A smell captured the feeling of a moment forever. Van Houten's hot chocolate will always be the warmth of my mother. The smell of fresh wild chives was a Sunday morning walk in Fort Tryon Park with my father—and always would be.

"Paradise Lake—City Limits," the discreet wooden road sign read. I turned to Mickey and blurted, "We're here!" Several hotel station wagons were waiting at the bus stop, each with its distinctive name and symbol.

"There's Ron," Mickey shouted, leading the way out of the bus. "He's the owner's son—a real cool guy." I followed and found myself with four elderly Europeans watching Mickey and Ron exchange warm greetings. After some brief introductions, all seven of us crammed into the white "Crystal Arms Hotel" station wagon and chugged off on a rocky dirt road lined with milkweed. I was struck by the "CA" logo adorning the car doors and was sure that, while never having seen even pictures of the hotel, it was inappropriately ornate. I was anxious to prove myself right.

The air was hot. All the windows were down and the road dust passed right through the car. I didn't mind. As we passed a cow pasture, the smell of cow manure also passed through. I loved it. To me that was summer. Freedom and summer rolled up in one smell. Glorious cow shit!

As we crossed over a small wooden bridge, Mickey turned to me and pointed, "That's it over there, across the lake—the white glob." My heart started to pound as the reality of this new experience hit me. The approach to the hotel was up a steep incline lined with pine trees and ended in a flowered cul-de-sac. I could almost see the history of the hotel unfolding before me. One unrelated addition after another had been glopped onto the original stucco fortress leaving the impression of a huge, lame white octopus. Most incongruous of all was the elaborate entrance canopy, probably tacked on simultaneously with the dubbing of the "Crystal Arms Hotel". I felt somewhat smug just then about my original reaction to the logo, yet was awed with the beautiful grounds and lakeside setting.

When the car stopped, I saw Mickey helping some of the elderly passengers with their luggage and automatically grabbed the remaining few bags. "I'll get those!" Mickey shot sharply, almost knocking me over. Stunned, I handed him the bags and meekly followed the entourage into the hotel.

A dank, yet comfortable smell greeted us new arrivals as we entered the expansive, though low-ceilinged lobby. The creaky wood floor was covered with many throw rugs of varying shapes as well as overstuffed couches and chairs. The room was quiet except for the lazy hum of a vacuum cleaner attended by a maid in a far corner. Two women were behind the reception desk busily shuffling room cards. As our group approached, the older of the two, a bespectacled yet attractive woman in her late forties, scampered out from behind the counter. With outstretched arms and a broad smile she echoed, "Hello, hello, hello," hugging one of the elderly newcomers.

The old man smiled shyly and said in a strong Russian accent, "It's been a whole year, Mrs. Miller."

Turning to Mickey and me while still embracing, she said, "You know, boys, the Barofskys have been coming here for nine years."

Feeling awkward, not having been introduced, I simply nodded, trying to look impressed while Mickey managed a "How are you, Mrs. Miller?"

"Fine, Mickey. Good to see you. Why don't you take the Barofskys' and Levis' bags and help them get settled." There was authority in her voice despite the smile and the slacks and the turbaned scarf. She turned to her son. "Ron, is this the new busboy?"

"Yes, Mother. This is Phil Dechter."

"You look like a nice young man. Why don't you go see Mr. Arthur in the dining room over there," she said to me, pointing to a pair of tall French doors. "He's the maitre d' and will tell you everything you have to know." I thanked her politely, then picked up my valise and trudged toward the appointed direction. The dining room was large and orderly, yet friendly. Full-height windows stretched across two walls allowing the noon-day sun to penetrate and creep along the bright red carpeting. Blank white tablecloths covered round tables arranged in staggered rows as if an oversized game of checkers was about to begin. All was quiet except for the faint tinkling of glass in one corner of the room where a hunched, middle-aged waiter was busy polishing his goblets.

I called out, "Excuse me. Is Mr. Arthur around?"

Without looking up, the waiter answered in a tired European accent, "Yeh. He's in de kitchen. He'll be out in a jiffy."

"Thanks." I fidgeted nervously with my belongings while looking around, trying to find some clue to what my job would be like. The "OUT" door from the kitchen suddenly burst open with a loud creak and an elegantly large, silver-toupeed man in a black tuxedo emerged.

"Are you Mr. Arthur?" I asked.

"Yes, I'm Mr. Arthur," he answered, looking down his narrow, pinched nose.

"I'm Phillip Dechter. I'll be working this week-end as a busboy and uh…Mrs. Miller told me to see you…." The scent of cologne hit me before any response from the older man.

"Well, yes. We are trying out a few new boys this week-end. It seems we always have a hard time getting our regulars at this time. The college boys are forever studying for examinations. This will be a good opportunity for you, young man. What's your name? Dechter? Ever work before?" his steel gray eyes never meeting mine. Just like Sharman, his compadre in Toupee City, he seemed to already know the answer and so continued, "You'll work with Sam…. over there. He'll teach you the ropes. We're only having two stations open this week-end so it should be easy for you. Come with me. You'll meet Sam." Mr. Arthur led the way with me following, struggling with my gear and stumbling through a maze of chairs. The waiter was still attending his goblets, stoically, yet lovingly.

19

As we two approached, he looked up slowly through heavy-lidded, long-suffering eyes and smiled softly.

"Sam, this is your busboy for the week-end…. Dechter?" the maitre d' said.

"Yes, Phil Dechter. How do you do?" I extended my hand eagerly.

"I do too much, but maybe now you'll help me a little, ay?" Sam responded with a benevolent twinkle, offering a warm handshake.

"Take him into the kitchen, show him around and get him some lunch. Then set him up in one of the bunks. He starts at dinner tonight." With that, Mr. Arthur did an about-face and marched off to the lobby.

Feeling awkward, yet trying to be friendly, I turned to Sam and asked, "He doesn't waste any words, does he?"

"That's his way of not getting too chummy, you know. But you and I will be friends. We have to be friends, or else our people will starve. Right, Philly?" Sam followed with a clownish shrug.

"Right!" I took an instant liking to Sam. After a moment's pause, hopefully to allow some rapport to set in, I frowned, trying to gain his confidence. "Listen, Sam…. I've never worked in a dining room before and I want to do a good job. You'll really have to start from scratch with me…. I'm sorry," I added sheepishly.

"Don't apologize. Listen, I've had to teach new kids in the middle of a meal. Don't worry. You look smart. You'll catch on. It's very simple. I bring them the slop. You take it away. That's the whole business. Come, I'll show you the kitchen. Then we'll talk over our own slop. Alright?"

The kitchen was a rustic space with most surfaces of white painted pine boards. Several tables, including the serving counter, were covered with faded oilcloth. The windows and outside doors were screened. Flypaper was hanging everywhere. Despite the fact that two people were working feverishly behind the counter, the room had the feeling of being deserted. Sam introduced me to Wanda, the fifty-ish Hungarian head chef and Max, an aging Chinaman who doubled as the second chef. Wanda greeted me warmly but impatiently in her broken English while Max merely grunted a reluctant "Herro." They were very much engrossed in their preparations for the next meal. Sam gathered us some warmed leftovers and led me to one of the oil-cloth-covered tables. As we ate, Sam described how the kitchen worked; what was where, and who was in charge of what. "Whatever you do," he said, looking at me sternly, "don't mix the meat dishes with the dairy. Boys have died for less. In a kosher kitchen, no matter how sloppy, that is a no-no. Some people get very upset if that happens and just won't forgive. So be careful, please—for my sake."

After finishing lunch, Sam led me up four flights of steep, rickety, flower-carpeted stairs to the top floor of the hotel where the dining room help slept. I was shown a small room with two bunks, a green dresser, flypaper and narrow window overlooking the garbage pick-up. Sam told me I would probably not have a room-mate for the week-end so I could really stretch out. Sam would not be sharing accommodations because he stayed in a small cottage behind the hotel where he kept his family the entire summer. He had to leave now but I was to meet him in uniform in the dining room at 5:00 P.M.

It was now 2:30. I was excited and quickly unpacked my few belongings, washed up and put on my uniform. As I attached my snap-on black bow tie in front of the small cracked mirror, I thought, "What a shmuck—I hope everyone looks like this." I tried catching a sideways glimpse, hoping to find a redeeming image. Even jutting my chin didn't give me much consolation. That damned seersucker shirt looked so much like seersucker. I knew I had some time to kill so decided to explore the premises. As I bolted down the stairs I could sense the hotel gaining occupants. Suitcases were stacked at ends of corridors, waiting for a frantic Mickey to take them to their assigned rooms. The lobby, too, had quite a lineup at the counter—and suddenly I felt a funny sensation in the pit of my stomach. Could I handle all these people? Was I going to make it through the first meal?

"Hey, busboy! Hey, you!" I felt a gentle tap on my shoulder, and as I turned, saw a smiling, redheaded, brash looking, slightly plump, but appealing late teen-ager. "You look like a busboy, but you sure don't know it," she continued, still beaming. "I'm Joann Miller, the owner's daughter."

"Hi, I'm sorry," I said, trying to recover. "I guess I'm not used to being called a busboy—yet. Just give me one meal under my belt, then watch out," I chuckled. "By the way, I'm Phil Dechter."

"Bye, Phil," she flirted, as she darted behind the counter to greet guests.

"Aggressive little thing," I thought as I headed toward the nearest door, hoping to escape, yet still observe the turmoil. I found myself on a long arcaded porch, crowded with empty rocking chairs and overlooking a marvelously clear, kidney shaped lake. Following my first impulse, I headed towards the water. The path was circuitous, meandering through several stands of tall evergreens, and ended in an open lawn sloping down to the water's edge. I felt a sudden surge of quiet freedom as the soft grass gave way to my heavy steps so used to the unyielding pavement of New York's stubborn streets. Alone for the moment, I smiled, allowing the peacefulness of the country setting to register. The smell of pine needles was everywhere. I inhaled deeply and stretched my arms to the sky, letting the warmth of the afternoon sun penetrate the thin membrane of my closed eyelids. I tried to imagine spending the whole summer here—who I'd meet, how the water would feel—whether anything would make a difference. After a while, I walked to the end of the wooden boat dock and perused the meager collection of rowboats bobbing lazily in the mirrored lake. Looking down, I hoped to see a sunfish or even a minnow, only to catch the reflection of Phil the Busboy. "That bow-tie looks so dippy," I thought, as the reality of the situation reappeared and a wave of anxiety again gripped my stomach. Walking back along the water's edge, I was annoyed that my enjoyment of the lake should be compromised by the uncertainty of my new experience.

As I approached the dining room, I saw Mr. Arthur sitting at a small table with a smart looking, well-endowed forty-ish woman who I later found out to be Sylvia, the hotel's hostess. They were reviewing the seating arrangements for dinner and ignored me as I slipped by through the French doors. Sam was sitting at his station smoking a cigarette while studying the menu. Without looking up, he said, "Dinner should be a snap. No choice on the appetizer—everyone eats gefilte fish. Only some will want the soup, but watch the soup—it's hot and it has waves…"

I interrupted, "What do you mean, 'It has waves'?"

Sam slowly shrugged his shoulders and intoned in his unending singsong lament, "Somehow the matzoh balls always make the soup dance around—but don't worry. I bring it to them. You only take it away. By that time the matzoh balls are gone. They always get the matzoh balls," he sighed. "But the soup is still there and it's still hot. They leave the soup just to see if you can take it away without burning them. But don't burn them. It makes them nervous. Besides, you'll get stiffed."

"What do you mean, 'Get stiffed'?" I asked innocently.

Sam rolled his beady eyes impatiently. "Stiffed, dummy! No tip! No money! Stiffed, get it? You come here to get tips, no? You burn the guest, you get no tip. It's that simple. So watch the soup, okay, boychik?"

"Okay."

"Anyway," Sam returned to the menu. "After the soup, we have a choice of roast chicken, boiled chicken, or flanken. Some choice."

Dinner turned out to be nothing like what I expected, even though I had absolutely no idea what to expect at all. I watched nervously as people started to file into the dining room. As Mr. Arthur steered a couple in my direction, the first to be seated at my station, I gulped hard then nodded with polite distance. Sam, on the other hand, embraced the couple, sat them down, and with one arm still around the man's shoulder, motioned for me to come over.

"Phil, I want you to meet Mr. and Mrs. Adler. I want you to know that I've served these wonderful people for the last four years and that they're very special people." Turning to the Adlers, he added, "Phil is going to take real good care of you. Aren't you, Philly?"

"Sure am," I answered, dutifully smiling at the non-descript Adlers. All the while, the remainder of our four tables were filling up, leaving thirty goblets in need of ice water.

The next forty-five minutes were a total blur as I found myself racing back and forth to the kitchen. Dirty dishes, clean dishes. "Yes, ma'am." "I don't know, sir." "Oops!" "Sorry, ma'am." "Right away, sir." I didn't see much of Sam, but somehow the food was getting to its destination. As I was pouring one of the last cups of coffee, I noticed Sam joking with one of the guests. "How could he do that?" I thought. "Stand there and talk to these people while I'm sweating my ass off here?" Without turning around, Sam gestured to me with a wide sweep of his hand, offering another cup of coffee to his companion in conversation. I obeyed dutifully while Sam continued his laughing banter.

When all the diners had left the hall, Sam sighed heavily and unclipped his bow-tie, lighting a cigarette in a simultaneous motion practiced over many years of repetition. "So, boychik," he said, releasing a long stream of smoke from his nostrils, "now you are a busboy. You did real good. How did you like it?"

I answered sheepishly, "It was rough," but decided not to complain any further.

"Rough?" Sam queried in disbelief. "You call that rough? You don't know what rough is. Let me tell you another thing." His voice suddenly became a little reproachful. "I've been watching you. While you're running around thinking how rough your little job is, your sour puss is telling everyone how you hate what you're doing. People don't like that. They want you to love them. They want you to love the half-eaten eggs they've spit out. Listen to me, boychik." Sam spoke softly now with his arm on my shoulder. "I've been on this earth a long time—longer than many of my friends. I know my people." He paused to light another cigarette. "I know you don't give a damn about these people. You're not going to wait tables all your life. You're going to be what—a lawyer?"

"No, a doctor."

"A doctor, no less." Sam rolled his eyeballs. "Well, my friend, you still have to care about people, or at least," he added with a gleam in his eye,"you have to make them think that you care. And besides, it's good for tips! Come, let's clean up and get out of here."

We set the tables for breakfast in silence. As Sam held a goblet up to the light to check his polishing skill, I noticed for the first time the ominous blue engraving of five numbers on his right forearm. A chill rushed through my body. I had heard about them, but had never actually seen them. So, Sam was a survivor. Here was the proof, the memory, never to be erased. With five lousy numbers, he was branded like a pig for the rest of his life. A concentration camp survivor. I felt embarrassed, hoping Sam had not noticed my eyes' direction. Should I say something? What could I say? Better not.

We left the dining room just after 9 o'clock. Sam advised a good night's rest since breakfast would probably be a "doozey." I was tired but not ready to go back to that tiny, lonely room just yet. I thanked Sam for seeing me through the meal, waved a weary farewell, then wandered into the main lobby. It was very quiet, yet as I looked around, virtually every seat was occupied. People were sitting in groups but very little conversation was going on. I felt as if I were invisible, traveling through a slow motion dream. Suddenly I was jarred by the sound of a pert, "They're digesting their food." I turned to find Joann Miller smiling at me, again with that flirtatious coo.

I blushed at having my unasked question answered and repeated timidly, "They're all just digesting their food?" We both laughed.

"It's a quiet crowd," she said with distant deliberate sophistication. I could sense she was trying to impress me. "Things should liven up once the season starts," she added, then slowly made her way back to the office, maintaining eye contact longer than necessary. I watched her full blue-jeans swagger away and disappear behind the counter and fantasized briefly about her potential in the sack. I then continued through the lobby, becoming increasingly self-conscious, not only of my stained seersucker shirt, but of my being one of the few mobile objects in the room. From out of the mass of quiet digesters, a pair of vaguely familiar eyes met mine and smiled. I surmised they belonged to one of my guests and, despite my natural instinct to glance away, found myself walking over.

"Good evening, sir," I said politely, not knowing the man's name. "Did you enjoy your meal?"

"I did and I didn't," the man offered philosophically, his round apple-face beaming benevolently. I was already sorry I asked. "The soup was hot," he continued, "the chicken was good, but....," after a long hesitation, "I like my tea *with* the meat, not after. Maybe tomorrow you'll be a good boy and remember. Okay, my friend?" Still beaming, he added, "You're a nice boy. What's your name again?"

I forced a smiling, "Phil, Phil Dechter."

"That's nice." The round face suddenly became very serious. "By the way, Phil, in the morning, could you please have a glass of prune juice waiting for me at the table." Then, almost pleading, he added in a whisper, "It's very important for me, you know."

"Sure thing, sir." I started to back away before more goodies would be heaped upon me. Did I have to put up with this shit after hours? "See you in the morning," I said, smiling.

I made a quick exit onto the porch where the cool night air welcomed me to the serene world of non-conversation. I hopped down the steps, relieved to be free of the staleness of the lobby. The moon was full and seemed to lure me down the road where the silence was even more enticing. I remembered the road coming into the hotel earlier that afternoon, which at this point seemed light years ago. The sound of crickets beckoned me to yank a weed from the side of the road and stick it between my teeth. So I wandered in the direction of town, my hands in my pockets, my bow tie still firmly anchored to my open seersucker shirt.

Reflecting on the happenings of the day, I decided I liked Sam, thought him wise, and wanted very much for him to like me. Perhaps Sam could see my foibles; he had already hit on what my mother had been bugging me about for years, what she called my "negative outlook". I knew it, disliked myself for it, but couldn't seem to change. Why couldn't I be happy-go-lucky like Johnny Singer whose parents have all the money in the world. But then again, I was better looking than Johnny Singer and did better with the girls.

It seemed extremely peaceful walking down this strange road, almost as if it were an unknown friend waiting for me to make my first appearance. My thoughts went back to the dining room. There had been another station working that meal, yet I had not said a word to either waiter or busboy. I should have gone out of my way to be friendly, I thought. Perhaps tomorrow morning would not be too late.

I now crossed a short wooden bridge leading into the town proper. The sound of water trickling over smooth rocks below now dominated the night air. I turned onto Main Street, which, but for the name, would have turned me elsewhere in search of the heart of town. The street was lined with small shops, dark and lifeless. Had it not been for the full moon, I would not have found my way at all. In the distance I saw a pair of elderly men strolling with their hands behind their backs, but that was it. This was Paradise Lake—another euphemism like the Crystal Arms Hotel. What was I doing here—in a deserted town in the middle of nowhere when I should be studying for those damn exams. I should not have listened to my friends—or my mother. Just then, I passed a large storefront window which looked like, if ever it were open, the local ice-cream parlor. The sign above the awning declared, "Poppy's". I looked deep into the dark glass, only to find the reflection of the same confused busboy I had seen earlier that day in the lake. I checked my chin, then my whole profile, hoping to find some comfort there somewhere.

# CHAPTER 3

The alarm clock startled me and sent me into a panic. Where the hell was I and shouldn't I be somewhere else by now? I looked at the clock, then fell back on my pillow. Slowly I ventured a peek out the open window. It was 6 o'clock and the sun was barely creeping over the mountains, causing large stands of pines to cast extended shadows over the terrain. The fresh smell of morning mountain air was invigorating, yet tainted by the sweet odor of decaying garbage lying in the trash containers below. I shaved and dressed quickly, then bolted down the stairs, eager to start the new day right.

When I arrived at the kitchen, I found Sam seated at one of the long tables in the middle of the room, drinking coffee and chatting with the two dining room guys I vaguely remembered seeing the night before. I grabbed a glass of orange juice and bowl of hot cereal and joined the threesome, anxious to be part of whatever camaraderie that was to emerge from this uncertain weekend. Sam looked up and in mock disbelief announced, "Well, my sleeping beauty has awakened to join the working class. Welcome!"

"Hi. Am I late?" I asked hesitantly, knowing that I had just blown my cool entrance.

"No, Philly boy—just kidding. Meet your fellow slaves, Murray and

Myron." The three of us nodded and shook hands awkwardly across the soiled table.

"Murray and Myron," I repeated. "That sounds like quite a team. You guys ought to go into vaudeville".

"Not really," Murray responded slowly. "We've got to get our act together right here first," with which he gave his busboy a nasty side-glance.

"He's just sore at me 'cause I dropped a tray last night," Myron said, a guilty gaze developing on his face. He was a skinny, freckle-faced kid about my age, with long gangly limbs and large dark friendly eyes. Almost by contrast, Murray, in his late twenties, was heavy set with thinning hair and bland features. He looked serious beyond his years, with a permanent frown engraved on his forehead. He smoked intently as we sat, more interested in the dangling ashes than the people around him. I decided that I was not going to like this guy at all.

The kitchen door flew open and a cheerful Mrs. Miller stormed in. "Alright, boys, the banquet's over. We've got people to feed out there." All four of us quickly got up, Sam and Murray crushing their cigarettes in their coffee grinds.

As we cleared our dishes, Sam looked at me sharply and said, "You pour the water. I'll get the butter and rolls." It was as if someone had pushed a button, causing everyone in the kitchen to move automatically. Even the dishwashers who hadn't as yet received a single dirty tray, acted as if the meal were in full swing. Mrs. Miller had that effect over everyone—always smiling yet making sure they knew who was boss.

When we were at our station in the dining room, I turned to Sam while filling the goblets with ice water. "This guy Murray doesn't seem too friendly, does he? Looks like he's giving Myron a hard time."

"Murray's alright. He's had some bad times." Eyebrows arched, Sam asked rhetorically, "Would you believe that the two of them worked together all of last summer?"

"You're kidding!"

"Murray needs a whipping boy and Myron Smith, who is not too bright, needs a master. It's a perfect team." Sam shrugged philosophically. "Don't worry about it. We've got people to feed here in five minutes," he added, imitating Mrs. Miller.

Just then, I remembered my conversation in the lobby the night before. "Sam, there was this guy in the lobby last night—one of our guests—I don't know his name and I don't remember where he sits, but he wants prune juice waiting for him at breakfast. What do I do?"

"You use your noodle, that's what you do. Go get the prune juice and put it at the station. Keep your eye on the door and when you see him, you give him a present. He'll love you for it. It's as simple as that," Sam shrugged.

"Thanks, Sam," I managed, dashing into the kitchen for the prize.

Mr. Arthur opened the French doors at precisely 8:00. Six elderly people slowly followed the swing of the doors into the dining room and proceeded toward Murray's tables. I watched with arms folded as Sylvia led another couple in, also towards Murray's station. My eyes fixed on Sylvia's full blouse, bouncing gracefully as she strode between the tables. "Amazing," I thought. Casually, I turned to my waiter and asked, "Sam, tell me, if Mr. Arthur is the maitre d', what exactly does Sylvia do?"

Sam smiled slowly and answered, "She does a little of everything. She helps a little in the office. She helps a little in the dining room. And she helps a little in the casino, sometimes even sings a little." After a pause, he added, "Mainly, she gives us alta cockers something to look at. Know what I mean?"

"I know what you mean," I said, disappointed that my discovery was shared with others.

Perhaps a dozen people were now approaching my station. I smiled good-mornings as I frantically scanned their faces, looking for the prune juice man. He was not among them. Probably stuck on the can somewhere, I thought, irked that I should have to worry about the man's regularity while my tables were filling up. I approached the first table where six guests were settling in and offered fresh coffee to "start the new day." Surprised at my own friendliness, I thought I might pursue a little light banter. I addressed the person looking the most responsive. "Looks like a gorgeous day. Do you have any plans to make the most of the morning?" As I asked, visions of last night's morgue scene in the lobby came to me and I was sorry I opened my mouth.

"Why of course, Phil," came the reply from a perky, if elderly pigeon of a woman with cheerful creased eyes and wide bands of gray wire hair separating a natural halo of orange. "Mr. Brickman and I plan to walk three miles after breakfast. Isn't that right, Herm?" She smiled, tenderly locking arms with her husband. He popped his bulbous eyes in mock surprise and declared stoically, "She's the boss. If she says 'three miles', then three miles it is. Maybe I should skip the pancakes."

While pouring the third cup of coffee, I heard Sam bellow from two tables away, "Good morning, Mr. Shulman!" I turned, and yes, it was him. I quickly set down the coffee pot and raced over to my bussing stand. I plucked the prune juice from its hiding place and presented it to Mr. Shulman just as he was sitting down.

"Have a pleasant morning, Mr. Shulman," I grinned.

I actually enjoyed the rest of breakfast, though constantly busy, clearing plates, pouring coffee, getting an extra dish of this or that—but it flowed. It was almost as if the arrivals, demands and ultimate departures of my guests were well-choreographed. They left satisfied and I felt, for the first time since my arrival, a real sense of accomplishment.

When the doors closed at 10:00 I yelled to Sam, "You're fantastic! How'd you know Shulman was my man?"

Sam shrugged coyly, "I know constipated when I see it. Listen, we're a team. When you need something, I feel it. When I need something,....soon you'll feel it."

"That sounds like I missed something," I said, somewhat deflated.

"You're doing fine, boychik. Getting better all the time. In another week, you'll be perfect. You're green, but you're smart. You're catching on. Some kids never learn," Sam added, tilting his head in Myron Smith's direction. "I like the way you're warming up to the people. Very important. If they like you, they'll forgive your mistakes. Be a nice boy. It doesn't hurt," he shrugged benevolently.

I was clearing the last of the dishes when the French doors burst open and a laughing Joann Miller came striding in, arm in arm with a stocky, fifty-ish man in a business suit. His authoritative gait, more than his resemblance to Joann, told me that this was the hotel's owner, Mr. Milton Miller. Sam greeted him warmly and asked about his drive up from the city and whether he could bring him some breakfast.

"Just a cup of coffee for me, Sam, thank you. I believe my daughter has already eaten." He spoke in a friendly but distant voice, his small pencil mustache reacting to each articulated word.

Joann steered him in my direction and announced gaily, "This is Sam's new busboy, Daddy—Phil Dechter."

"Pleased to meet you, young man," he said, extending his hand.

"My pleasure, sir," I replied, shaking hands. I noticed Mr. Miller's glasses had very thick lenses, distorting his eyes into a constant half-smile expression. It was difficult to read this man.

"Phil's a Columbia man," Joann interjected. "He's up for the weekend but will be back for the whole summer."

"Oh, very nice," the owner said politely. "What are you studying?"

"I'm a pre-med. I mean, I'm studying the Humanities right now and hope to go to medical school after that."

"Very nice," Mr. Miller repeated blandly, turning his attention to his coffee.

When the two had left the dining room, Sam turned to me with a twinkle, "Someone's got a crush on you, Philly boy, and I don't think it's

Milton. I think that someone wants you around for the whole summer, too. You heard her tell her father."

"I hear you, Sam. I just wish she weren't so damn obvious. Tell me about Mr. Miller."

"He's a big man. I mean he's a big man in New York. A lawyer. A corporate lawyer, whatever that is. Milton comes up on weekends when he can. Usually lets the Mrs. run the show. He's a nice man, very gentle. But once in a while he gets mad—then watch out. Once he fired four waiters and busboys just before dinner. Why? Because they weren't clean-shaven. He never cared before. That night he cared. Everyone begged him to change his mind, but he wouldn't budge. He served all the guests himself—and they loved it. After the meal, they clapped for him. He's a bit of a showman. The whole family is. Anyway, be nice to Joann. It will pay off for you."

That evening the guests dressed a little more formally than before. It was Saturday night and there was a show in the casino. I was anxious to see what kind of scene that would be, perhaps a clue to the entire summer. I rushed through the after-dinner clean-up and asked Sam if anyone was going downstairs for the show. Sam declined himself, saying he would rather relax with a cold beer in his own cottage, but added that I would probably find the others there. In fact, I would most definitely find Myron Smith. I raced up to my room, washed up, shaved, and put on one of my two clean sport shirts. Just as I grabbed my tweed jacket and was about to leave, I spotted my soft-cover version of Camus' "The Stranger." I had brought it this weekend to read in my spare time. In fact, I had taken that book on several trips for the same reason, but never seemed to be able to get into it—but it always looked good under my arm. At that particular moment, I was hoping I would once again not have to be returning to my last resort.

Passing through the lobby, I found the guests more actively involved in conversation than the night before, and most everyone seemed to cast a pink glow, a benefit of the day's benevolent sunshine. I went to the lower level and meandered around the lounge, hoping to find a familiar face before venturing into the darkened casino. The curved walls were faced with a shiny star-glittered wallpaper, punctuated every few feet by signed photographs of smiling entertainers, the names of whom meant nothing to me.

Feeling I had loitered long enough, I pushed through the casino doors, finding myself in a virtual sea of blackness. After a few moments, I began to discern small flickering lights coming from netted bottles on round cocktail tables scattered about the large room. A round wooden dance floor separated a raised bandstand from the seating area, at this point not quite half filled. I sat down at one of the tables, still trying to accustom myself to the darkness. Immediately, I was greeted by Mickey the bellhop, who at this hour was playing Mickey the barwaiter. He informed me that if I chose to remain at the table, I would have to tip. Otherwise, I would be better off joining Myron Smith over at the bar. Miffed at Mickey's crudeness, yet thankful for the information, I made my way over to the bar where a smiling Myron Smith lit up, "Hi ya, Phil. You down for the show?"

"I guess so. What goes on down here?" I asked rhetorically.

Behind the bar, a huge hulk of shirt emerged from a crouch and, still wiping his hands from handling crushed ice, smiled at his two patrons. "Hi. You boys drinking tonight?" I saw a corpulent, forty-ish body topped by a round red baby-face. The bartender could not have been over thirty. His long black hair was slicked back in a duck's ass, with an appropriate cascading curl down his forehead.

"Sure, Terry," Myron Smith answered first. "How about a beer, Phil? By the way, do you know Terry the bartender? This is Phil the busboy."

Extending my hand, I was met by a still ice-cold, yet friendly firm grip. "Yeah, I'll have a beer," I said. "You know, I feel like I'm in a Damon Runyon story. Everybody's got a title. I'm waiting for Gertie the gun moll to show up. Myron Smith almost fell off his barstool, thinking that was the funniest thing he had ever heard. Terry smiled again, then fetched the two beers.

I gazed into the smoked glass mirror behind the bar and was surprised to find myself drinking a beer. I had never thought of myself as a beer drinker, especially not as one sitting at a bar. Yet here I was and the place was filling up.

The reflections in the mirror then yielded another familiar face, that of Joann Miller. She was wearing a blue cocktail dress and looked a lot more grown-up than in blue jeans. Actually quite attractive, I thought, though still a little on the heavy side.

A sudden drum-roll silenced the crowd, as Sylvia walked out into the spotlight and took the microphone. She welcomed everyone to the casino in a deep reflective voice tinged with a slight mid-European accent of indeterminate origin. She then began to sing a nostalgic ballad of that other world, "Wien, Wien, nur du allein........." I was mesmerized by what I thought Marlene Dietrich might have sounded like. The spotlight above made her white sequins dress glow, accentuating her ample, Rubenesque form.

"She's got great tits, don't she?" Myron Smith offered.

"Yeah.... You sure have a good eye," I answered, annoyed that I couldn't enjoy this vision of mature voluptuousness in peace.

Sylvia sang a few more sultry numbers, then gave way to a short round chunk of a man, bouncing onto the platform in a white tuxedo jacket and touting a large cigar. He reminded me of Mr. Sharman, the person who sent me into this strange world what seemed like four hundred years ago. Perhaps it was the obvious toupee or just the brash confidence exuding from such a stump of a man. He took a few long puffs on his cigar and watched, as his audience was forced to watch, the smoke rise into the spotlights. Then, introducing himself as Al Diamond, your master of ceremonies, he proceeded to tell some off-color jokes, laced with country-Yiddish. I could understand only a small part of it, but the rest of the crowd loved it. The enthusiasm was reaching a fever pitch when he suddenly shifted gears and started to sing "My Yiddishe Momma." He had the audience so wrapped up that when he finished, they yelled for more. With a big sweaty bow, he promised to be back, then waved to the band to start some dance music.

The heavy beat of the cha-cha poured out as a few couples made their way to the dance floor. I looked around, feeling the urge to hit the floor myself. Spotting Joann Miller dancing with one of the older guests, I could tell that while she was moving slowly to accommodate her partner's pace, she was graceful and probably a good dancer. After waiting out a fox trot and a waltz, I heard the familiar introductory beat to "Cherry Pink and Apple-blossom White" and decided to make my move.

Joann saw me coming and stood quizzically with hands on hips. "Shall we...?" I asked simply, then led her onto the floor. Immediately finding each other's groove, we smiled confidently, easily dominating the dance floor. I enjoyed the knowledge of being a good hoofer, but it was Joann who started to strut her stuff by wandering all over the floor. Soon the other dancers gave way to us—and it was exhibition time. By this time I was sweating profusely, but loved every moment of it. Each time I made a pass behind her, Joann stretched her neck, maintaining eye contact, a move she made flow with her body rhythm. "Sensuous little tease," I thought, continuing to smile and gyrate. When the set was done, a round of applause greeted us as we made our way to the side.

"Want a drink?" I asked automatically, still somewhat out of breath.

"Sure! That was fun," Joann answered cheerfully. "Let's sit over at this table."

I followed uneasily, anticipating an encounter with Mickey. When the barwaiter did approach, Joann simply flipped, "Put this on my tab, Mickey. I'll have a rum and coke. How about you, Phil?"

"A gin and tonic would be great for me."

When Mickey left with the order, she began, "You're a real sharp dancer."

"You're pretty good yourself. Been entertaining this crowd since you were a kid, I'll bet."

"Sure have. I do a little singing, too. You'll see later. Look at poor Myron Smith over at the bar. He looks so lonely. Serves him right, actually. All he does is drool over Sylvia. He's a real animal. None of the girls will have anything to do with him."

"Other girls?" I asked coyly.

"There *are* other girls around here, don't you worry," she pouted. "During the full season we have a couple of girls behind the desk, a couple in the day camp, and of course, there's the rest of town. I'm sure there'll be enough girls to satisfy you."

I tried to shift the conversation to avoid her sarcasm. "Tell me, why does everyone call Myron Smith by his full name?"

Joann giggled. "Think about it. Say 'Myron' slowly by itself and think about it. Then think 'Smith'. Put them together and it's very funny". She giggled again.

I did as instructed, then smiled and said, "You're right. It is pretty incongruous."

Joann suddenly got very serious. "Don't use words like that around here. People don't like it. Not everybody goes to college and it makes them feel inferior. It's just a helpful suggestion. You don't have to take it. Once there was a snooty guy here from Princeton and he let everybody know it. The other guys in the dining room finally had enough and roughed him up. He left the next day. My parents don't know about that but I have my way of knowing what goes on." After a thoughtful pause, she said, "Anyway, it would be nice to have you around for the whole summer."

The drinks arrived.

"I'm planning on it," I smiled and raised my glass.

# CHAPTER 4

Memorial Day began with another beautiful sunrise. The morning was cooler than the two previous days, causing me to wake up early. I bounded out of bed and surveyed the landscape. This was the pay-off day, the wrap-up of my first weekend working the mountains. Sam had told me the money would come all at once, right after lunch. "Just stick around. Don't go hiding in the kitchen, and it will come," he said. I washed up, and as I shaved, found myself smiling back in the mirror.

When I arrived in the dining room, Sam was studying the seating chart. Without looking up, he announced that the Yaegers and the Shulmans were leaving after breakfast. "Be nice to them," he squinted through the smoke from his cigarette, "and don't let them out of your sight."

"Okay, okay," I responded. "By the way, what can we expect from these people for the weekend?"

"Phil, Phil, Phil," Sam shook his head slowly. "You mean it took you three days to ask? Let me put it this way. Basically, this is a 'schlock' house. It's a five and three crowd. 'What's that?' your puzzled face asks me. Well I'll tell you. For each person who stays a week, the waiter gets $5 and the busboy gets $3. Sometimes it's more; sometimes it's less. Sometimes when it's much less, the people have to be educated. That's right, boychik. Don't look at me like that. Sometimes you have to talk to them." He paused to let that unpleasantness sink in. "But don't worry," he continued. "Usually when the busboy gets stiffed, so does the waiter. I'll do the talking, but you've got to learn. Some boys are afraid to say anything, but they're fools, and I'll tell you why. We're not here for our health. We're here to make money. People should know that and understand it. Once in a while an old fart will come along who really doesn't know what tipping is all about. Who knows where he's been all his life. Anyway, you tell him—nicely, but you tell him……. Enough of a lecture. For this weekend, let's figure four and two. Okay? Let's go to work."

The doors finally closed behind the last of the lunch guests. I collapsed in a chair, too tired to count the money stuffed in all four of my pants pockets. I reached for the dish of apple strudel I had stashed away in my bussing station during the meal just for this moment. As I downed my treasured morsel in two gulps, I watched Murray and Myron Smith hovering in different corners of their station, counting their weekend's take.

"So, Philly boy, are you a millionaire yet?" Sam startled me, causing me to almost choke on my strudel.

"I don't know. I didn't get a chance to check yet," I answered, waiting for another fatherly admonition.

"You don't know? Here you are, starting a new career and you don't know if it pays?" Sam mocked.

I quickly extracted all the loose bills from my pockets and arranged them by denominations. "Seventy—six dollars," I exclaimed.

"Not bad. Not bad at all for thirty four guests." Sam raised his eyebrows, "I better watch my step or you'll take away my job." With that, he gave me a warm bear hug. "You did good, boychik."

Before Sam could release his grip, we were interrupted by the high-pitched din of a small dinner bell coming from the front of the dining room. Mr. Arthur was standing there in a tailored beige-tweed sport coat, cream colored dress shirt and white tie—with his Florida tan and silver coif—the epitome of the Esquire man—holding the bell. "Will all of you boys come over here for a short meeting," he said flatly. I was embarrassed to hear Sam included in the category of 'boys'. Surely Sam had at least five years on this fop. "Except for clean-up," he began, "the weekend is essentially over. It went fairly smoothly. Of course, there's always room for improvement. I'm happy to announce that you've all been asked to return for the summer season,"he announced unhappily.

"Who's this guy talking to?" I thought to myself. "I'm the only one who hasn't been here forever. Why doesn't he just say that?" I looked around and found the others staring at me. I felt obligated to say something. "That's great," I began. "Thank you very much....... When should we be back?" I asked hesitantly, feeling very vulnerable.

"You'll all report on the Thursday before the July 4th weekend. Sam, of course, will be staying on." With that, the dapper maitre d' turned and exited through the French doors. It was as if the curtain had fallen at the end of the first act of a plotless play. The four of us watched in silence.

"That fuckin' bell!" Myron Smith broke the spell. "I was sure he'd lose it sometime over the winter."

# CHAPTER 5

The bus ride home seemed a lot shorter than the one out. The good parts of the weekend ran through my mind again and again. I hadn't known what to expect, and it turned out well. At least I had a job. I was set for the summer—unless I really screwed up.

As the bus entered the Lincoln Tunnel, the reality of the present sunk in. Now I knew exactly what to expect. I had precisely two days to cram for that CC exam and knew I wouldn't be seeing a pillow during that time. Dancing butterflies began to coat my gut.

Emerging from the subway, I was welcomed by a soft breeze bearing the friendly scent of my slowly decaying neighborhood. It seemed as if I were gone for a month, not a weekend. I walked the three blocks to my apartment building briskly, anxious to share the weekend with my parents and sister.

"So? How's my working son?" My mother greeted me at the door with a big hug. "It looks like the fresh air did you some good. You have nice color in your cheeks. Put your bags down and tell me. Was it as terrible as you thought it would be?" She smiled, rubbing my hand warmly the way she had done hundreds of times over the years, whenever she wanted to be particularly proud of me.

"It was great. It really was," I said, withdrawing my hand. "Where's Lisa and Pop? I might as well tell all of you at the same time."

"Daddy's out for a walk. He should be home soon, right before supper. Lisa won't be home. She's out auditioning for another play."

"Damn. She's never around when I want to talk to her. I'll get rid of my stuff in the meantime and wash up. You know I'll be up all night studying for Tuesday's exam."

"Don't blame me for your tests," she shouted in her Viennese accent. "If you have a job for the summer, you should thank me for pushing you. You'll study and you'll do fine. And you'll have a job—if you have a job. Why you have to wait for Daddy to come home before you tell me, I don't understand." She huffed into the kitchen.

Supper was one of my favorite's—wiener schnitzel with rice and fresh peas, and cold potato salad soaked in olive oil. The three of us sat at the red and white oilcloth covered kitchen table, enjoying whatever late spring evening air filtered through the billowing sheer curtains from the air shaft outside. "Well, I think I've got a job for the summer," I began. I then went on to describe the weekend in detail. Fred Dechter listened eagerly as I spoke, living each moment as it was retold. My mother, on the other hand, was less interested in the details as she was in the results. Her son made $76 for the weekend and had a summer job to look forward to.

As I licked the last of my chocolate eclair off my fork, I frowned and turned to my father. "Did you know there were places like the Crystal Arms and whole towns catering to refugees? You must've."

"Sure we do," he answered, glancing uneasily at Helena Dechter. "We know a lot of people who spend their vacations in Paradise Lake. If you're asking why we never went there, it's very simple. We don't like living in the past. It hasn't been that good to us."

# CHAPTER 6

Driving my father's car and taking Carol to the year-end Tau Alpha Pi bash held particular promise that night. While sitting next to her always felt good, Carol's extra dose of my favorite scent gave her round forms a special aura of accessibility. That and the relief of having just finished the last of my final exams made me feel almost euphoric. We spoke casually of our summer plans and how we would write regularly. We had been dating fairly steadily since February when Carol and some of her friends had visited the fraternity (never call it frat) house on a Friday night Open House. I had been immediately attracted to her fresh open face and voluptuous body.

I had many friends in TAP, but was embarrassed by the feeling that I hardly knew the majority of my "brothers" and probably never would. I disliked a whole group of upper classmen because they regarded my pledge class as lowly freshmen, not worthy of sharing the same room with them. I often wondered why I went through the degrading process of pledging just to be called a brother to these assholes. But I had done it because it was the thing to do and had made good friends among my pledge class. Perhaps it was the mutual survival of hazing that formed the bond between us.

All the lights of the three story limestone townhouse were blazing when we arrived. Silhouettes of young people partying could be seen in many of its windows. Jerry Arnold, the official fraternity greeter, was at the door, drink in hand, and pearly whites aglowing. "How ya doin', Phil ol' buddy? I see you've got your best lady in tow," he said.

"You got it," I smiled, hating every word coming from this patronizing viper of an upper classman. To my relief, I spotted Bruce Klein, the pledge class clown, entertaining two girls in the foyer. Seeing me and Carol, Bruce stopped mid-joke, and skipped over.

"Hey, Phil baby, we actually made it through first year! It's all over now but the alphabet soup. I heard you're going to the mountains this summer.... Hey, Carol," he turned, pretending fear, "you'd better watch this tiger. I hear the women are pretty wild up there."

"I've got my spy system all set up, thank you," she smiled.

Bruce Klein was slightly built and had a bad case of lingering acne. Yet his large, twinkling dark eyes and quick wit won him great popularity in the freshman class. "Not to change the subject, but to change the subject, I've got this great bit to put on for the brothers during the presentations." Glancing coyly at Carol, he added, "I hope the ladies present won't be offended."

"Knowing you, Brucey," I said, putting my arm around my diminutive friend's shoulder, "there's no chance they won't." All three of us laughed and went into the great room.

At about 11:30, Paul Samuelson, the fraternity president and undisputed B.M.O.C, stepped in front of the still-glowing fireplace and gave his wine glass a few taps with a spoon. Within moments the room was silent. Couples necking in various corners and couches of the room looked up in the half-light to see what cool Paul Samuelson had to say. My thoughts darted to the Crystal Arms Hotel where I envisioned Mr. Arthur ringing his ridiculous little bell. How foolish the man looked compared to smooth Paul Samuelson. Silhouetted against the orange flames behind him, Samuelson was the dream of every co-ed in the room. He was, likewise, the hero of his peers.

"Ladies, gentlemen,...and brothers," he began. "I trust you're all enjoying yourselves, this being our last party of the year. It's been a great year—one filled with many challenges and successes. I, for one, will miss you all next year. The house, the parties, but mainly the people. But we've gotten a lot of good new blood this year, so I know the brothers will carry on...... Speaking of carrying on, I know there's a guy in this room who really knows how to carry on. I present to you—Bruce Klein."

Hoots and hollers filled the room as Bruce stumbled his way to Paul's side. "Thank you, Paul. As always, you're a hard act to follow," he giggled. "As all the brothers know, first year English is no picnic. But some of it stuck. In fact, I composed a little poem I would like to share with you all— in the style of the classics—to glorify our loved ones.... if I can find it." He groped through all of his pockets and finally found a small crumpled piece of paper. "Here it is. I call it,.......'*Ode to a Ginch*'

*O glorious female, chewer of Beechnut gum,*
*How I long for that sixth day when once again*
*You appear, oh lovely dragger of heels;*
*For God created you on the sixth day,*
*And you appear on that day from then hence forth.*
*O essence of womanhood, retainer of that original fruit,*
*How my heart throbs for that part closest to yours.*
*How your bouquet radiates, o wearer of knee-socks.*
*How you vibrate, o tight-sweatered lassy.*
*You are the most chaste of maidens, o teaser of tools.*
*Your beauty was matched only in the days of old*
*When famed Socrates was the prize of all men.*
*O lover of rhythmic music, connoisseur of fine pizza,*
*O pure and innocent one, uncorrupted by worldly culture,*
*O beloved Ginch, hailer from FAR-ROCK-AWAY,*
*Famed Lorelei, reclining on a FAR-AWAY-ROCK,*
*How I, the Horn of Plenty, Reaper of many harvests,*
*Long to plow your fertile field of fruit."*

Somewhere amidst the uncontrolled howling that followed, I heard Carol whisper, "I think that's disgusting."

"Aw, come on, it's funny. It's really funny. Where's your sense of humor?" I laughed uncomfortably.

Carol got angrier. "I suppose that's the way you feel about me. If you remember, that's the way we met. You know, there's definitely a lack of respect for women around here and I don't like it one little bit. I think I want to go home."

The drive home was quiet, lacking the fulfillment the early evening promised. When we arrived at the door to Carol's apartment, we looked sadly at each other for a long time. Then I broke the silence. "I'll call you before I leave for the mountains." Then I turned without a touch, and left.

# CHAPTER 7

I put my valise and satchel down on the sidewalk and instinctively looked back up toward the third story windows of my family's apartment. Sure enough, my mother was peering through the sheer curtains. "It's all right," I yelled up to her in exasperation. "We already said goodbye. I'll write you in a few days." I threw up my hands and walked to the edge of the curb trying to ignore my mother's protective gaze. After taking a deep breath I looked up to the clear sky, remembering a similar day when I took my first step to becoming a rookie mountain rat.

A bright red Chevy Impala convertible screeched up to the curb, forcing two young children to scurry to safety. Joann Miller waved from the driver's seat, her silk scarf billowing in the breeze while her eyes twinkled behind her almond-shaped sunglasses. "Welcome aboard the Crimson Chariot."

"Thanks. It's real nice of you to give me a lift," I said as I put my belongings in the trunk. "I really wasn't expecting the offer last week. This sure beats the bus."

"It was nothing at all. Between my house and the mountains, I was headed in this direction anyway," she beamed.

Tooling up the New York Thruway, the red Chevy passed every vehicle on the road. "You like to drive, don't you?" I asked.

"I can be pretty fast when I want to be."

"You can also get a ticket doing that, you know."

"Maybe yes, maybe no, but only when I drive," she purred. I smiled quietly behind my sunglasses, cupping my hands behind my head and gazing skyward.

The Crimson Chariot set its sights on its next victim—a convoy of three busses, each affixed with a banner reading, "Camp Tiroga Bound." As she passed them, Joann let out with a disdainful laugh, "Ha! That's Tiroga, a camp outside Paradise Lake—for brats only!"

Unknown to me at the time, the lead bus held a group of eight and nine year olds singing campfire songs led by two counselors. One was a long rangy youth with short cropped hair and swarthy complexion, looking as if he had just ambled off a basketball court. The other was Laurie Stillman. Her bouncy, cheerleader good looks had the added dimension of her dark intelligent eyes which darted smilingly from child to child. Her softly athletic body swayed to the rhythm of "Workin' on the Railroad" as her blond ponytail kept the cadence. Laurie Stillman had been a camper at Tiroga for six summers and loved it. Now she was coming back as a counselor after several years' hiatus, one as a foreign exchange student in the Netherlands, and the last taking summer courses at Hunter College. Perhaps it was her infectious enthusiasm, perhaps the contour of her T-shirt. By the time the bus exited the Thruway at Kingston, every fourth-grade boy in her charge had fallen in love with her.

# CHAPTER 8

"We're home," Joann chortled as the car came to an abrupt halt behind the hotel. In front of us, three young men were removing their gear from the Crystal Arms station wagon parked at the rear entrance. She called to them, "Hey, you guys the new dining room staff?"

They looked at each other for a moment as if to assure one another of the validity of their common description. The shortest of the three finally responded. "Yeah, I guess we are. Who the hell are you?"

"I happen to be the owner of this hotel," she retorted with overzealous indignation. "And my friend here is a veteran busboy."

I smiled impishly and approached them. "Yeah, I've cleared a few meals in my day. Hi, I'm Phil Dechter."

"Hi," said the red-faced short guy. "I'm Danny." Then in a whisper, "Is she really the owner?"

"Yup! That's Joann Miller," I said with confidence. "Get used to the idea of having an extra boss around."

The remaining two introduced themselves. Bobby Meyers, a ruddy kid with sparkling gray eyes and in need of a shave, was the taller. The other was Sid Goldhammer, a pale owlish fellow, several years his senior. As we shook hands, Myron Smith yelled from the porch above, announcing that Mr. Arthur had called for a meeting of all dining room staff immediately.

Before I could scurry off with the others, Joann held back my arm and said, "I like the way you handle yourself, busboy."

"Thanks, boss."

".... four, six, eight, nine." Mr. Arthur counted heads quietly, ignoring the bodies to which they belonged. Then addressing the group in general, "Is someone missing? There should be ten of you."

"I heard one guy cancelled out," Murray explained.

"Damn!"

"That's okay, chief. I like to work alone." All eyes turned to the source of this panacean offering. We found a well-built, stocky sort with close-cropped curly black hair and deep-set, almost imperceptible, tiny dark eyes. I saw a big rat wearing a white shirt and black bow tie.

"I'll decide if anyone works alone," Mr. Arthur darted back. "And while I'm at it, let me set the record straight. I'm addressed by one name and one name only—that is to my face—and that is 'Mr. Arthur'. I am not your friend. If you play it right, I will not become your enemy. And remember this: I always win." He paused, making eye contact with each member present, then continued. "This is a business and there's plenty of money to be made. Those of you who have worked with me before know how I operate. The others will learn. I'm fair to everyone." Letting that sink in, he added, "Cheating and thievery will not be tolerated. If I hear about it, you'll be out of here before the next course is served. Of course," he paused with a hint of a smile, "I'm sure you have your own means of maintaining fair play in the dining room. Isn't that right, Mr. Simon?"

"I suppose so," a tall blonde athletic type responded nonchalantly.

"Well, let's get on with it," Mr. Arthur continued. "Each station is responsible for its own silverware. You'll get your allocation now and it will be up to you to keep track of your numbers. Silver will be polished at all times and lord help the man who mixes meat and dairy. The station assignments will be as follows: Koenig will work with Smith; Simon with

Meyers; Goldhammer with.... Danny?.... Don't you have a last name?"

"Yeah, but Danny's okay. There aren't any other Danny's around here."

"What's your last name?" Mr. Arthur asked impatiently.

"Fishwasser."

"Thank you, Fishwasser. That's very good. Goldhammer and Fishwasser. If you gentlemen don't make it in the dining room, you might consider opening a law firm. Well, anyway, to get on with it, Sam will work with Dechter, and for the time being, Gould.... Is that your name?"

"Yes, Mr. Arthur, Marty Gould," answered the massive rodent.

"For the time being, big mouth, you'll operate alone, but only temporarily. Now, all of you, get your stations prepared and be back in the dining room ready to work at 4 o'clock. That's all I have. Koenig will answer any questions." With that, he abruptly exited through the French doors, leaving the staff to size one another up.

I looked around. The guys seemed all-right...except for that Marty Gould character. There was something scary about him that I could not put my finger on. Sam leaned over and whispered, "Divide and conquer, that's his tactic."

"Who?"

"Arthur, dumbchik. He does it every time. He doesn't want us to trust each other. That way he keeps control."

"Is there reason not to trust?" I whispered back.

Surprised by the question, Sam nodded, "Unfortunately."

Murray Koenig broke the silence. "In case any of you new men didn't catch Mr. Arthur's drift, he doesn't like to be bothered with questions. You come to me with your problems. And although he didn't say it in so many words, let me make it clear. I'm first station.....And don't give me that smirk, Stan."

Stan Simon smiled broadly as he continued to rock on the back two legs of his chair with his hands clasped expansively behind his head. "I didn't say a word, my captain."

"The chief didn't say nothing about a first station. As far as I'm concerned, we're all equal," Gould blurted.

"Ease up, new guy. It's not going to make any difference to any of us," an annoyed Stan Simon offered. "Just stay cool and stay clean and you'll make out just fine. In fact, if you play it right, you might even win the coveted KMA at the end of the summer like our fearless leader Koenig did last year."

"What the hell's that?" Gould challenged.

"*That* is the Karl Miller Award—for obedience, named after the old man's old man," Simon responded. "It's also known as the Kiss My Ass award, for obvious reasons. But it's worth fifty bucks to the guy who can stay with it for the duration." Silence.

Standing up and taking a long playful bow, Sam broke the awkward tension in the room. "Now that we're all one happy family, let's get to know each other and then get to work. I'm Sam Schectman and I'm not going back to college in the Fall." Everyone laughed at the old man's good-natured self-deprecation and slowly began to mingle.

"Hey, guys," Stan called out, "we've got almost two hours before we really have to get back here. Any takers for a little half-court basketball out back?"

"Cool and clean," I thought. That was Stan Simon to a tee. Sure, I would join him. We could all use the relief.

Ten minutes later, four lean bodies were sweating eagerly over a large brown ball on a broken asphalt patch behind the kitchen. Bobby Meyers and I were the "shirts". The taller Stan and shorter Danny were the "skins". The players were all new to each other but we all loved the game. Stan dominated the court, not only with his height and strength, but with his ability to find Danny, whose outside shots never missed the basket. Bobby and I were capable shooters but no match for this Mutt and Jeff combination.

"Hey, you guys are too good," Meyers said panting and throwing his hands up as if to surrender. "I heard you were pretty good, playing for N.Y.U. and all," nodding to Stan, "but the little guy is too much. You sure you guys never played together before?" Laughing, we all slumped down under a large oak tree and stretched out under its welcome umbrella of shade.

"Danny reminds me of this guy at Columbia, Chet Forte. Five foot six and scores forty points a game," I mused. "He's got this fall-away jump shot no one can stop. A real phenom. I wonder if he'll make it to the pros."

"The only thing your friend and I have in common is height," Danny lamented. I can't even make it to the amateurs. I'll be lucky if they let me back into Brooklyn College in the Fall."

"You know," Stan started as he gazed up at the tree, "for a guy who doesn't seem to like anything about himself, you're a pretty funny man. I'll bet you could make a pretty good living just making fun of yourself."

Danny responded by flicking an imaginary cigar and raising and lowering his eyebrows a la Groucho Marx. "I may not have much of a choice."

As we walked back, Bobby Meyers broke the joking mood. "Hey, Stan?" he asked, scratching his dark stubble, "you and Murray don't seem to get along too well. What gives?"

"Well, my man," Stan chuckled as he put his arm around Bobby's sweaty shoulder, "let's just say we've known each other a long time—maybe too long. As much as I hate to admit it, we're cousins. Yup, we actually share the same grandmother. I still consider him a schmuck, and if you ask him, he'll probably call me a real prick."

"So you guys are really very much alike, after all," deadpanned Danny.

\* \* \*

"We're here because we're here because we're here because we're here.......!" Jubilant echoes rocked the quiet of the pine setting as the buses churned up the dirt road leading to Camp Tiroga. Young heads stuck out of open windows while wild hands pointed at familiar landmarks.

Hy and Bea Rappaport stood at the flagpole waving warmly to "their" kids as the buses came to a halt. Young campers scrambled off, shuffling their possessions and jockeying for position among their peers. Laurie Stillman ran to the Rappaports with open arms, a broad smile spreading across her radiant, tanned face. The camp owner whirled her full circle with a bear hug. "We've waited too long for you to come back to us," he said, his white teeth flashing to match his flowing hair. "You don't know how happy we are to have you again."

His wife stepped up, a wide grin pasted on her face. "You were always such a precious little girl. Now you're back as a young lady, prettier than ever."

"Listen, I'm a counselor now—with kids to watch over. That's why you hired me, remember?" she laughed. "So, gotta run. See you later." Laurie dashed off.

"I hope Jack sees what we see," Bea Rappaport sighed to her husband. "He'd be blind not to. I just hope he doesn't let every other counselor at her first. Sometimes he can be so damned passive. I don't know where he gets it. Certainly not from me."

# CHAPTER 9

Mr. Arthur escorted the last of the dinner stragglers through the French doors and into the lobby. As soon as the doors latched closed, Bobby Meyers fell to his knees, threw his hands up to the ceiling, and declared in mock hysteria, "Man, we gotta get outa here!"

"Amen," responded Myron Smith. "That was one tough meal."

"Ease up, busboys," Stan interjected with a lopsided grin on his face. "The fun is just beginning. Tell you what I'm gonna do. Whoever can finish up and be ready to go in fifteen minutes can hop on my wheels and go to town. I'm ready to explore the terrain. Any takers?"

"You're on!" screamed Danny, as he burst through the kitchen door with a tray full of freshly washed goblets.

The clean-up pace quickened. I remembered seeing Stan's black '49 Ford coupe out back and wondered if there'd be room for me. I really wanted to go. It would be the first real excursion and Stan would be the right guy to be with. I begged Sam to finish polishing my goblets, then raced upstairs to change. Bobby Meyers was already in front of our shared mirror, powdering off his upper torso, having just treated himself to a hasty whore bath.

"If you want to go, Phil boy, you'd better forget about washing up. Douse yourself with this cologne. That'll kill the sweat. I'll save you a seat in the back. Hurry!" With that, Bobby dashed out of the room, buttoning his shirt as he ran. I did as instructed, then grabbed the first sport shirt in my drawer. As I tucked it into my pants, I realized it was the wrong one— not my lucky shirt. But it was too late. I had no time to change now. As I bounded down the stairs, I felt an uncomfortable, sticky sensation between my skin and the unloved shirt.

The car was already idling when I reached the lot. Sid and Bobby Meyers scrunched over to allow me to park half a cheek in the back seat. Myron Smith and Danny were already in the front with Stan. The door slammed, rubber peeled, gravel flew, and the evening had begun.

The ride to town was quiet. Everyone in the car was aware that six unwashed bodies were trying to make it to town with limited cover-up devices, and each member of the conspiracy was hoping that his own defense would not be the first to go. A few casually raised arms and quick sniffs confirmed the concern.

Unlike my first impression of Paradise Lake, the streets were now teeming with life. People milled under lamp posts and in the streets, ignoring the honks of cars trying to make their way through. Stan, however, had a way of maneuvering through the crowd in a "take no prisoners" fashion. The Simobile, as his car was soon to be dubbed, found a small spot right in front of Poppy's, where it banged its way between two parked cars to a place of temporary rest. The sidewalk throbbed with groups of teens and college age kids, some still wearing the black and white vestiges of their mountain rat uniforms. Eyes checked out other eyes as well as anyone entering the portals of Poppy's. Encouraged by the scene, Stan let out with a "Let's go get 'em" cheer and led his crew into the action center of summertime Paradise Lake.

Johnny Mathis greeted us at the door with "Chances Are" blaring from the jukebox in the haze of the backroom dance floor. The front portion of the shop was a cake and ice cream parlor, a respectable daytime attraction for the European set, while the younger generation took over the back at night.

The Crystal Arms six strutted into the back room and jostled our way across the dance floor to one of the few remaining vacant tables. The room was oval-shaped with rustic wood beams overhead and knotty pine wall paneling. However dim, the lighting did not fail to reveal the multi-engravings gracing each wood table, accumulated over many years of waiting for drinks to be served. Sid Goldhammer, the bespectacled and scholarly looking law student from Cornell speculated aloud about a particularly bold carving, smack in the middle of our round table. "'Shelly and Poochie, 1955'. Now there's a pair. Who do you suppose was who? Shall we take a vote? All in favor of Shelly being the male, say 'Aye'." Four loud "ayes" resounded.

"Hey, guys," Danny protested in his high squeaky voice. "I kind o' think Poochie's a neat name for a guy."

"Yeah, probably a guy from that camp up on the hill," added Myron Smith. "Those counselors always have those cutesy names."

"Why don't you ask them?" Stan cut in impatiently. "There's a whole table of counselors from Tiroga right over there." The other five pairs of eyes jerked in the direction indicated. We found a group of eight wholesome looking preppies thoroughly involved in a funny story being told by one of its members. My attention quickly riveted to a blond ponytail dancing joyously with the laughter. I could not see the owner's face, yet my heart began to beat thunderously in anticipation. Then, just as the jukebox started to play "Cherry Pink and Apple Blossom White," she suddenly got up and, with a gangly crew-cut type in tow, approached the dance floor. She smiled as they cha cha'd, and even in the dim light, I could see her perfect white teeth flash winningly across the room. "She's absolutely beautiful," I thought, oblivious to the idle chatter at my own table. I still could not see her features too clearly and yearned to be closer. But I was paralyzed. Perhaps it was my shirt that was surely reeking by now, or maybe just my innate tentativeness. And damn it, she was dancing with someone, anyway.

A thirty-ish waitress finally appeared at our table. "Hey, I remember you from last year," she said, her eyes twinkling toward Stan. "You gonna behave yourself this summer?" she asked with a burst of bubble gum.

"Of course I'm gonna behave myself. Don't give my friends here the wrong impression," Stan answered with exaggerated hurt. "Look, honey. You owe me an apology. But I'll tell you what. I'll settle for a round of beers on the house." With that, he rocked back on his chair and started to howl. We all joined in, eager to get into the spirit of the place.

"Here we go again," the waitress said impatiently, rolling her eyeballs to the ceiling.

Sid broke the stalemate. "Just bring us six beers. We'll haggle price later."

"Hey, I like your style, four-eyes," offered Danny, as the waitress huffed off, shaking her head.

"A little more respect for our lawyer friend, young Daniel," Stan chided. "He's gonna represent the dining room staff in all our future labor grievances."

Sid's eyes creased behind his horn-rimmed glasses as he immediately responded, "After much deliberation, I respectfully decline. I have other previous commitments."

"Such as what?" Bobby demanded.

"Such as polishing silverware,…. and keeping my job so I can go back to school in the fall." We all laughed, but nodded knowingly. I was still mesmerized by the graceful form on the dance floor.

"See anything you like, Phil boy?" Stan asked paternally.

"There's a lot of nice stuff around," I answered as generally as possible.

"Tonight, we look. Next time, we attack," Stan said gleefully. The waitress returned with six Buds. Stan raised his glass. "Here's to our summer. Let each of us find what we're looking for."

"Here, here!" the rest of us chanted, and raised our glasses in unison.

# CHAPTER 10

The week that followed was one of establishing routine. Each team of waiter and busboy got to know each other's quirks, strengths and weaknesses, and found intuitive ways of compensating for one another. Only Marty Gould remained a one-man show, a force without alter-ego. He went about his business quietly and efficiently—almost too efficiently. No spare words were exchanged with the rest of the dining room staff and no love was lost in the process. He was consistently the first one out of the dining room at night and not to be seen till the next morning. Murray Koenig, who considered himself a deputy in charge of operations, often complained about Gould's lack of cooperation. No one disagreed, yet no one could put a finger on just what was wrong with this loner. Even Mr. Arthur, who had a nose for sensing hostilities, insisted that a busboy was coming up to balance out the stations.

Sam and I were working well together. We found a groove each of us could live with—one which boiled down to mutual respect. With his sage philosophy, almost in spite of himself, Sam was slowly becoming another father figure to me. Wanda had also taken a shine to me, often finding a special dish or seconds for one of my guests when the supply had supposedly run out. As for me, I felt I was quickly learning—even the devious tricks which made work a little easier. Like the morning I was asked for a glass of freshly squeezed orange juice. I ran into the kitchen and asked aloud to no one in particular, "Where the hell can I get fresh orange juice?" Murray quietly pointed to an open coffee can filled with orange pits. I unhesitatingly grabbed a handful and tossed the pits into a glass of the regular watered down frozen juice variety. The guest was no wiser, in fact, happily commented on how fresh it tasted.

The tips coming in the first week were lower than anticipated, based on head count. Sam explained it away as being natural for the early summer which usually attracted a cheaper crowd. Yet, Thursday morning, as we were setting tables for lunch, I turned to Sam and confided, "You know, Sam, I was just talking to Stan and Myron Smith. They both worked here last year and said tips were better then. They can't understand it. If I don't start to average $3 a head, I'm going to be in trouble."

"Don't worry, boychik. You're doing a good job and the tips will come. Don't be so impatient." Then he added, "Listen, my friend, I know you've been working hard. How about you and me relax with a little schnapps together in the bar tonight—my treat. You can't beat that, can you?"

"You're on, boss. Best offer I've had yet."

* * *

Shortly after 9 o'clock that night, I walked into a virtually deserted casino bar. The only discernable sound was the shaking of a mixed ice drink Terry was making for some invisible patron. Sam was sitting at a small corner table quietly smoking a cigarette. He wore a clean white short-sleeved shirt, just as he would in the dining room, but I knew it would be fresh. Sam seemed to wear nothing but white short-sleeved shirts, but would save the white-on-white prints for non-working hours. He rose as I approached and extended his hand in a friendly, yet formal man-to-man fashion. I realized, with all the intense and interdependent time we spent together, that this was the first time we were meeting in a non-business setting.

"So, Phil, we meet outside of the trenches," Sam began, reading my mind. "What would you like? I'm having scotch and soda."

"Gin and tonic would be just fine for me, Sam."

Sam ordered the drinks from Mickey, then smiled at me, "You having a good time so far?"

"You mean tonight or the summer?"

"The summer, the summer, not tonight, dummy! How can you have a good time sitting alone with an old fart like me?"

I laughed. "You know, you happen to be the funniest guy around here and I'm also learning a hell of a lot from you. I'm really glad we're working together."

"Boy, oh boy! You buy a kid a drink and he tells you you're wonderful. I should do this more often." The drinks arrived. Sam raised his glass and twinkled, "L' Chayim." I responded in kind.

A round beaming face on a wall poster smiled down at us as we took our first sips. The poster declared, "Gala Dinner To Honor Mayor Rudi Ostheimer, July 15, 1957." Sam looked up at the poster and raised his glass again. "L' Chayim to the mayor."

"Do you know him?"

"Yes and no. Everybody knows Rudi. He gets around." Sam downed his drink and ordered another.

Feeling that Sam wanted to talk but seemed to be closing up, I prodded, "Tell me about your family."

"Ah, my family! My wife Esther and my daughter Shana—she's six— they're just down the road at our cottage. But of course, you haven't met them yet. You will, soon. You're surprised that an old geezer like me has a six year old child. Well, I'll tell you……" He paused and drank half of his second scotch without interruption, then continued. "My little Shana is my life." He stopped again and finished his drink—then looked at me strangely. "This is not my first family. I had another family once. It seems like one hundred years ago, but it was maybe only fifteen or twenty. I had a beautiful wife and three fine boys. This was in Poland. Then came Hitler and he changed the world.... Why am I telling you this? You don't want to hear it. You're here to make money and have a good time."

"Please, Sam. I really do want to hear about it." I was earnest in my pleading.

"Well, things moved so fast. People couldn't believe what was happening. One day, I'm happily running my little restaurant—see, I'm still in the food business. The next day they throw me out and I'm being 'relocated' to an unknown place. Some things are a blur, other things I remember like it happened this morning. I was still with my family on that train. We huddled together, not knowing what would be next. And then the worst happened. When we got to where we were going—Auschwitz, they separated us. I never saw my wife and sons again..... I'm drinking too much. This is depressing even me."

"Please go on." I could see the torment in this poor man's eyes.

"They put me to work, so I worked. This is some union card they gave me," Sam said, showing me the blue numbers etched on his forearm. "I don't hide them. I'm not ashamed of them, but there is shame here. Now, I call these numbers my 'receipt.' I lost my family and my living—and somebody owes me. But I don't know who. God, maybe.... Anyway, I was at Auschwitz till the end of the war, surviving as best I could. Then a cousin I had in New York helped me come here. For years I tried to find out what happened to my family. I finally gave up. Then my cousin brings his cousin Esther to meet me. And soon we got married. And now we have Shana and she is life for me. You see, Phil, I'm a quiet survivor." Sam looked up again at the smiling face on the poster. "You see him? Now he's a good survivor!.... I know him better than 'yes and no'. You see,...Rudi and I were at Auschwitz together. For two years. We lived and died together. That was thirteen years ago. What's thirteen years of freedom compared to one day in Hell?" Sam paused to compose himself. My heart was pounding. I had never heard a first-hand account of any of the Holocaust and was fascinated by it, almost in a ghoulish way. Yet these were my people.

Sam continued, "Now we don't talk. Rudi is busy with his success and I mind my own business..... No, it's more than that. We can't talk. It's too painful. If we talked, we would both cry. When we see each other, we look the other way. Maybe that's good. On the other hand, when all the Jews with numbers on their arms are dead, there will be nothing to remind anybody. This must not happen. We must not forget. You, boychik, must not forget. You're young and you must remember." Sam realized he was pressing my arm and backed off slightly. Then with a twinkle in his moist eyes he said, "I better not hear from anybody about Rudi and me or I'll kill you.... Or worse, I'll cut off your tips. Understand?"

I smiled and yes, I did understand.

# CHAPTER 11

The midmorning sun streaked through the windows of the dining room, silhouetting Mr. Arthur against the shear curtains. The assembled staff squinted as we heard him begin, "So you boys aren't happy with your tips. I called this meeting because some of you are grumbling that you're working for nothing. I'm not unsympathetic, if that's the case. I also won't have our guests abused by ungracious employees." He looked around his dining staff, waiting for a reaction. "I'm a busy man. I don't have all day to cater to a bunch of moody busboys."

"Busy shtupping Sylvia, I'll bet," Myron Smith whispered to me.

Murray Koenig stood up and responded to our leader. "Perhaps I can put this in perspective, sir. Because I've got first station, some of the guys think all the big tippers are being assigned to me."

"Bullshit!" interrupted Stan.

"Save it, Simon. You'll get your turn to speak," the maitre d' interjected calmly. "Go on. Koenig."

"First of all, it's not true. And my tips have been pretty shitty too. To prove it, I'd be willing to pool tips."

"No way! I wouldn't trust that snake."

"Shut up, Simon. We're trying to hold a civilized meeting here." Mr.

Arthur was determined to maintain control. "What do you think of the idea of pooling tips, Sam?"

All eyes turned to Sam. His face wrinkled into a quizzical expression as he slowly shook his head from side to side. "Personally, my friends, I don't think it's such a good idea. Honesty is a virtue and I'm sure everyone here has at least a little of it. But honesty is also fragile, and sometimes when you have a dollar bill in your hand and you've earned it, it's hard to let go. And you know what the real problem is? I'll tell you. It's not dishonesty. It's suspicion. Nobody wants to be a dope. If you think somebody else is pocketing money, why should you make a donation? No, my friends, it's really a terrible idea. It may be sad but there are very few angels left on this earth, and I doubt very much if they're all concentrated in this dining room. I think we'll all stay good friends if we keep our own money."

"Amen," clapped Bobby.

"Now, Simon, what do you have to say?" asked Mr. Arthur.

"Not too much. Sam said it all," he sighed.

"Anybody else? How about you, Gould?"

"I'll get by," he grumbled. "Why doesn't everybody just mind their own fuckin' business? Since when is this a socialist state?"

"That's enough," interrupted Mr. Arthur. "It seems that the pooling idea is not getting much support. Does anyone have anything constructive to say?"

"Yeah, maybe," offered a pensive Sid Goldhammer. "I thought we were trying to increase tips here, not just share the lousy tips we're getting now. Last summer I waited at a lodge in Fleischmanns where they had a sign that just might do the job here."

"What'd it say, 'Trick or treat?'," Danny broke in, starting a chain reaction of laughter.

"Dammit!" shouted an impatient Mr. Arthur. "I don't give a rat's ass if you people make money or not. If you're serious about this, it seems to me that you owe it to yourselves to hear what the man has to say. Go on, Goldhammer."

"It was a very discreet sign—not offensive at all," Sid started again. "They hung it over the front desk and it said, 'MANY PEOPLE ASK US, "HOW MUCH....? WE CAN ONLY SUGGEST THE FOLLOWING TIP SCHEDULE.' And then it listed tips for everyone from waiter to chambermaid. It was really pretty effective. We all assume people know. Many of them don't or just forget from year to year. We can't just write everybody off as a stiff."

"He's right," supported Sam. "The people have to be educated, and maybe the sign can do it—if it's got the right numbers."

"Fine. I'll check it out with Mrs. Miller—see if she has any objections," offered Mr. Arthur with surprising encouragement. "In the meantime, is there anyone here who's halfway artistic?"

"Yeah," I volunteered to my own surprise. "I could make a decent sign."

"Mine own busboy—an artist," chortled Sam, "and he never told me." He shook his head in mock disbelief.

Before the laughter subsided, the French doors flew open and in strutted Joann Miller leading a lanky young man with a shock of straight blond hair and wearing a wide toothy grin. He carried a satchel similar to the one I bore the first time I crossed those same portals, except this one had stenciled across one side, in bold white letters, "Thomas L. Jamieson III." Joann paraded him right up to Mr. Arthur and happily announced, "This is the new busboy, Mr. Arthur. His name is Tom Jamieson and he's from Atlanta, Georgia." She accented his place of origin as if it were the moon itself.

"Pleased to meet you, sir," he drawled, extending his hand with an ever so slight hint of a bow.

"Holy shit!" Gould murmured in more than a whisper.

Mr. Arthur had no choice but to shake the hand of this stranger from a strange land. "Glad to have you aboard, Jamieson," he said stiffly. "You'll work with Gould over there."

"I told you at the beginning I like to work alone," Marty Gould protested. "I don't need nobody."

"Well, I think you do," the maitre d' cut in. "The crowds are going to start coming in and we need all stations at full strength. If you don't like it, you'd better tell me right now." When Gould said nothing, he continued, "Besides, all of you could probably learn a little about hospitality from our new Southern friend."

Jamieson, still smiling, but somewhat embarrassed by the proceedings, nodded with a "Hi y'all" to everyone.

"Well, that's enough of a discussion for now," the silver-topped maitre d' said as he prepared to leave. "Goldhammer, you put some numbers together for me to review, and the rest of you help out the new man..... One more thing. My bell seems to have disappeared. I want it to reappear before the next meal. That's all." Then he left.

Stan made the first move toward the new man. "Welcome to the north country, fella," he said warmly. Then in a hushed tone, "If that asshole Gould gives you a hard time, you let me know."

Most of us began to drift to our own stations. Joann followed me to mine and asked in a coy whisper, "Isn't he cute?"

"Who?"

"Tom."

"A real peach," I said sarcastically, then added more sincerely, "He seems nice enough. How'd he get up here, anyway?"

"His father's a business associate of Daddy's. They thought it would be nice for him to work the summer up here and get some experience— that is, until football practice starts next month."

"That skinny guy plays football?"

"Ooh, you're jealous, already. He's supposed to be fabulous. He plays tight end or something for Georgia Tech and has oodles of money."

"Terrific! Now that's a great combination. I guess I'm out of the running, Joann. I have no money and only play a fair game of tennis. Such is life." Throwing my hands in the air, I added, "Please leave me so I can cry in my goblets."

"Don't get so huffy," she said, somewhat hurt, and huffed off, swaggering in her tight jeans.

In the far corner of the dining room, Marty Gould went about his table preparations for the lunch meal, oblivious to his new busboy standing by, waiting for directions. Finally, Jamieson said with a big smile, "I'm here to help you, Marty. Just tell me what to do. I'm new at this game."

"Great!" Gould scowled to his silverware. "Now I'm supposed to teach the cracker from scratch. I'm doin' fine all by myself, then some rich southern boy waltzes in and wants to play busboy for kicks. I don't need this shit!"

The smile vanished from Tom Jamieson's finely chiseled face and his deeply set eyes intensified. He said, "Hey, guy, where I come from, a man gets a little more respect as a stranger. You don't know me and I sure as heck don't know you."

"This ain't your turf, country."

"That's for sure as shootin', city boy. But looky here. I'm here to do a job. I come in good faith; maybe not the faith you're comfortable with, but that's another matter. I'm real friendly and I learn fast, so why don't we just get on with it?"

I overheard the exchange and felt an instant admiration for the newcomer who had scored a put-down without the bully Gould realizing it. I had disliked Gould from the start, but now embarrassment was added to the negative vibes. Like it or not, Martin Gould was one of mine, one of the Jews who served the Jews in one of the few spots on earth where Jews dominated. And now a visitor from another tribe had come up to the mountain to dwell amongst us in peace, if but for a short time, and was being shat upon by an ill-chosen representative of the majority. If

Thomas Jamieson III became anti-Semitic as a result of his experience in the Catskills, I couldn't blame him. Gould could do that—even to a fellow Jew.

In the next few days, Tom did indeed learn the ways of the dining room, not through any effort on the part of his waiter, but with the help of the other busboys who found his smile and style most ingratiating. Though his presence lent a self-consciousness to the Jewishness of the rest of the staff, he was not considered an outsider, but a welcome novelty—to all but Marty Gould. Even the guests at his station took a shine to his southern grace and good manners.

Tom became a regular at the half-court basketball bouts, rivaling Danny's speed and quickness. One afternoon as the group lay in the shade recovering from a particularly grueling game, Stan asked him, "How can you work with that fucking creep?"

"Hey," he smiled, "I'm the outsider here. I know that. I appreciate what all you boys are doing for me, but listen. Who am I to judge my fellow man? If one of you boys come down to one of the clubs outside of Atlanta, who knows how you'd be treated. I've only met a few people of the Jewish faith before and I liked them just fine. I think this experience is just great."

"I just want you to know there aren't many of us around like Gould," Stan said. "If he were an Arab, I'd be a lot more comfortable."

Within two weeks, Tom was gone. Thomas L. Jamieson II had suffered a heart attack on the golf course and his entire family was summoned to his bedside. Tom got the call after midnight and left within the hour without goodbyes. A stunned staff heard the news the following morning and held a walking wake as everyone went through the motions of preparing for breakfast. "What a great guy," Myron Smith started.

"A true gentleman in every sense of the word," Sid Goldhammer added.

"Well, I never trusted him." Marty Gould broke the spell. "Their kind is just playing with us."

"You son of a bitch!" Sid yelled as he lunged at Gould.

"Don't give me that shit," Gould smirked, as he easily fended off his attacker. "So Tommy the second croaks. Tommy the turd is right there to take over in the boardroom. These guys have got it made so bad. You don't find no Jewish boy sitting so pretty."

Stan Simon gently put down his tray of assorted juices. He then grabbed Gould by the shirt, almost lifting him off the floor, and causing his bow-tie to pop off. "You're sick, man," he shouted. "You make me ashamed to be a Jew. Why don't you crawl back into your hole where you can hate yourself without affecting anyone else!"

The door to the dining room opened and Stan released his adversary. "Any problems?" Mr. Arthur asked innocently, as just his head appeared around the door.

"No problem," Stan sighed heavily. He then walked over to me and whispered, "We gotta get outa here. How about you and me taking off tonight and check out some of the other hotels?"

"Great! But tell me something. Are you a Psych major?"

"Yeah! How'd you know?"

"Oh, just a wild guess."

# CHAPTER 12

I stood on the west porch and watched the sun fade, then disintegrate into horizontal bands of vermilion. Slowly they dropped off, one by one, behind a skyline of far away pines. It had been a while since I had had a moment to drink in the beauty surrounding this crazy new world of mine. Then I felt a gentle tap on my shoulder. The finger belonged to one of my guests.

"Hi, Mr. Borensweig," I greeted warmly.

"I'm sorry to disturb you," the old man began, "but it's nice to see a young person appreciate nature." His narrow eyes twinkled in harmony with his thick Teutonic accent.

"It is beautiful tonight, isn't it," I agreed.

"The water reminds me a little of Lake Lugano in Switzerland. I haven't been there in twenty five years but some things you don't forget."

"I'd love to hear about it. I've never been to Europe but hope to get there when I'm out of college."

"Ah, to be young again," Borensweig said wistfully. "I would like to remember Europe the way it was when I was a young man—not the way I left it. I used to ski in the Alps before anyone ever heard of a chair-lift. And that was before the First World War, if you can believe it. I would hike all day with my comrades to the top of the mountain, and then, in one glorious swoosh, we would schuss all the way down. We only had one chance but we made the most of it."

"You're still in great shape, sir," I said, encouraging him to go on.

"For an old geezer of seventy-eight, you're right. God didn't mean for me to be fat, so he gave me this wiry body which I have used well. He also gave me a bald head at the age of thirty-five. I still can't figure out why." We both laughed.

A familiar car horn sounded three times, prompting me to beg my exit. "I'd really like to hear about your experiences, Mr. Borensweig, but right now my ride is here and I've got to go. Have a nice evening."

\* \* \*

"What took you so long?" an impatient Stan Simon asked when I reached the car.

"Hey, I was talking to one of my guests."

"Do you want pussy tonight or would you rather talk to an old fart?"

"I like the old man," I answered defensively. "Pussy's going to be around a long time. Mr. Borensweig may not."

"Okay, okay. Call me a horny Philistine and hop in."

"Where are we going, horny Philistine?"

"The Garlands! It's on the other side, but that's where the action is," Stan responded, flooring the accelerator to accentuate his point.

I sniffed around suspiciously. "What the hell are you wearing?"

"Me?" Stan asked innocently. "Just a whole bottle of a little something my girl gave me as a send-off before the summer."

"Does she love you or is she trying to get rid of you?"

"Ha! Hey, tonight's tonight. I really want to score. Are you ready ?…I mean, do you have a rubber?"

"Yeah, I've got one."

"Good. What kind of girls do you like, Phil-boy?"

"Oh, I'm not particular. They just have to be gorgeous and have great tits."

"Not bad, young man. Not bad at all."

"You think Tom will be back?"

"I don't know," Stan pondered. "He was a good man. You think they'd give us a trade? One goy for one Jew, even exchange?"

"Who would you have us give up, pray tell?"

"Are you kidding?"

Leaving the city limits of Paradise Lake, we drove east towards South Fallsburg, enjoying a brief period of silence. Stan then turned on the radio and Frank Sinatra immediately responded. Stan and I joined him in singing "All The Way," while opening the windows to allow the lazy cows in the nearby fields to relish the three voice harmony. The clean evening breeze flushed the car as its headlights aimed for the land of promise.

The main drag of South Fallsburg teemed with loud people wearing even louder clothes. A thin gauze-like haze, formed by the constant billowing of expensive cigar smoke, hung overhead, separating the street-borne humanity from the clear heavens above. The black Simobile inched its way among the pink and yellow convertibles as two mountain rats searched the throngs for worthy prey.

"What do you think of the crowd?" Stan asked.

"It sure ain't Paradise Lake," I answered, somewhat awed by the circus-like surroundings.

"If we can only get this buggy parked, we'll get right to it. The Garlands is just around the next bend."

Gorilla-like attendants in maroon monkey suits were checking cars as they drove through the main gate. Stan quickly put his car in reverse and made a screeching detour to the service entrance. "Why can't we go in the regular way?" I asked innocently.

"We're just scum-balls from another hotel looking for pussy. They don't want us—especially those assholes at the gate. If they knew we were here trying to score with their women, they'd throw us right out. We'll just go through the coffee shop and make like we work here. That's the beauty of the bigger hotels. Nobody knows who works where."

The corridors were lined with boutiques, paved with marble and adorned with walking furs. "It's the middle of summer. Why are all these women wearing fur?" asked a befuddled me.

"It's the uniform. In the army, you wear khakis. At summer camp, you wear week-end whites. In the mountains, women wear furs. It's that simple. They come with the Cadillacs," Stan answered matter-of-factly as he scanned the lobby for more interesting quarry. "Tell you what. There are two places here. One's the nightclub they call 'The Green Room,' where the big spenders go. They'll probably throw us out 'cause we're not wearing ties. But I think you'll get a kick out of seeing it. Then we'll get serious and go to the bar where the real chicks are." With that, Stan led the way toward a wide arcade more ostentatious than the other passageways. The marble floors became plush green carpet. The boutique fronts became gilded wall mirrors, and the bright lighting turned into subdued sparkles from a myriad of crystal chandeliers. At the end of the hall we were greeted by a series of double oak doors leading to the hallowed "Green Room," but not before being screened by another pair of tuxedoed gorillas seated at a gilded desk.

"You boys have a reservation?" one of them asked sweetly.

"No, but my friend's mother is in there and she has our car keys," Stan answered to my surprise.

"That's a good one," the other bouncer said sourly. "Only one of you can go in there—and make it fast. There's a show going on."

"Go on, Phil, it's *your* mother."

"Okay. I'll be right back." I went through the doors and was immediately hit by the blackness within. After a few moments, I could discern that the room was a huge semi-circle with stepped tiers of candle-lit tables leading down to a large stage. Through the haze of more cigar smoke, I guessed there were at least five hundred people. The spotlighted figure on stage was struggling to make the jaded crowd laugh at his crude Jewish jokes. Something wasn't reaching these people. Perhaps the acoustics were affected by the absorptive qualities of the two hundred fifty odd mink jackets draped over wrinkled but tanned shoulders. My pondering of the physical and meta-physical dynamics of the room was suddenly interrupted by one of my hosts who inquired if I had yet found my key-bearing mother. I told him I guessed she wasn't there after all and offered to leave this dark chamber of mountain culture.

After joining Stan outside, we began to sprint down the hallway, over the green carpet, past more furs, over the marble floors, past the boutiques, and through a dark wooden archway. Immediately we knew we had arrived in yet another world. We were in "The Sandtrap," where furs were replaced by sequined gowns clinging to young bodies with smooth skin.

The music, loud and infectious, seemed to penetrate every breathing object present, while the thick smoke quivered with each drum roll. All eyes were on the Frank Sinatra imitator belting out an open bow-tied "Witchcraft," thrilling the girls and giving cause for hope in every male in the darkened room. Stan ordered a couple of beers as the two of us sidled up to the bar, then elbowed me in the ribs with, "Check the two chicks at 3 o'clock."

I angled toward the designated coordinate and nodded approvingly, "Let's go get 'em."

The two girls were seated at a table by the dance floor, their silhouettes highlighted by the spotlights beyond. With a cigarette poised between her graceful fingers, the slender brunette nursed a gin and tonic. Her blond companion, fuller of form, stared into the smoke, mesmerized by the sweating, finger-snapping crooner.

"You girls care for some company?" Stan opened with a winning smile.

"Suit yourself," the brunette answered indifferently, glancing casually at her pursuers as we pulled up a couple of chairs.

"You could be a little more enthusiastic," I offered. "My friend Stan here drove up from the city this evening just so he could be here with you."

"Isn't that sweet," she replied sarcastically, cooly exhaling a stream of smoke.

I caught a twinkle of a smile from the blond, however, and turned my attention to her. "My name's Phil and you must be the friendly one in your social group."

She smiled again and said, "I'm Sandy, and this is Audrey." I was physically jolted by the sound of her voice. It came from the body of a woman but had the pitch of a thirteen year old and inflection from the bowels of Flatbush.

"Well, Sandy, where're you from?"

"Scarsdale."

Stan and I looked at each other. Either the girls were loaded or were trying to impress us. In either case, a round of drinks was in order—an investment of sorts. Stan asked a few casual questions regarding Scarsdale geography and possible mutual friends—enough to support his hunch that they were fellow cruisers. The band began to play a slow number, so I asked Sandy to dance, my license to test the silent language of pressures and responses. Her waist had just the right amount of give. It reminded me of Carol and gave me a pang of guilt, if but for a moment. I hadn't really thought of writing her anyway. Sandy returned my squeeze of hand, encouraging me to hold her tighter. Her hair was swept up high overhead, exposing dangling rhinestone pendants hanging proudly from her perfectly shaped ears. I could not resist blowing gently at the few stray blonde wisps crossing her suntanned lobes. She giggled softly.

When we returned to the table, Stan and Audrey were gone. A darkly unctuous bar waiter approached me with the check and a smirk. "Your friend left," he informed. "He said you'd take care of this."

"Right!" I said curtly with a frown, trying not to blow my cool. I threw a few dollars on the table and suggested to my companion that we get out of this dive.

Sandy's spiked heels beat irregularly on the pavement as we walked briskly across the moonlit parking lot—a strange counterpoint to the soothing sound of distant crickets. The otherwise stillness of the night was in great contrast to the man-made tumult we had just left behind inside the bar. Yet I wasn't quite ready to come up for air. I had a hot number in tow and had to move fast. If only I could find the car. Pulling her gently to the side, I leaned back on a nearby car and put my arms around Sandy's waist. We exchanged silent smiles as I planted a long kiss on the side of her warm neck, all the while trying desperately to remember the whereabouts of the elusive Simobile. Then a car door slammed and a partially dressed yet vaguely familiar form ran towards us. "They're animals," Audrey panted. "Let's get out of here!" She grabbed Sandy's arm and started to tug her away. Sandy looked at me helplessly as she staggered off with her friend into the darkness—and out of my life forever.

Stunned by the sudden and disappointing change of events, I managed to find the car and a hysterically laughing Stan within it. "What the hell did you do?" I demanded. "First you stick me with the check. Then you screw me just when I'm about to score. What gives?"

Still chuckling, Stan mumbled, "I simply asked the lady for a blow job," a new rush of self-amusement overcoming him as he slid out the door and fell onto the concrete. He looked up at me with glazed eyes and drawled, "I detect disapproval of my tactics from my Ivy League friend. Hey, there's no harm in asking. Tell me, Mr. Couth, how does one request a blow job at Columbia?" My anger melted as I looked down at my friend, sprawled on the ground like a helpless but playful puppy. A smile forced its way around my mouth, then a snicker, as I too got caught up in a jag of uncontrollable laughter. Two mountain rats found themselves howling at their own ineptitude while the moon watched stoically overhead.

# CHAPTER 13

As a sign, "WELCOME TO PARADISE LAKE" was not memorable, but tonight it was a sight for bloodshot eyes as two returning warriors crossed the bridge into town shortly after eleven o'clock.

"Well, you win some and then you lose some more," Stan said wearily. "It's like a batting average. If you hit .300, it's not so bad. Wanna call it a night?"

"You think anything's happening at Poppy's?" I asked.

"We won't know unless we're there. Let' go."

It was less crowded than the last time we edged our way to the back room. Stan looked for a table. I searched for a blonde ponytail. Stan found his mark. I did not. We slumped into our chairs and scanned the social terrain. In despair, I called for a couple of beers. The music was right—but no ponytail. Then I heard a laugh I had heard before and my heart jumped. It was her, but without a ponytail. Her silky hair just fell lazily on her shoulders. I laughed giddily to myself. Hey, she wasn't obligated to wear a ponytail forever just so that I could identify her. She was gorgeous either way—any way. Now what? I'm here. She's there. I had just returned from a full circuit of the Catskills looking for what was just thirty feet away. Even the Platters were doing their part with a slow ballad. If only my heartbeat could keep pace. Suddenly she got up and started for the door. Involuntarily, I found myself following her. I caught up to her and blurted simply, "Are you leaving?"

Surprised, she turned and smiled, "No," then continued out, leaving me totally perplexed. Not wanting to look like a world class fool in Stan's already blurry eyes, I ambled around the entry area pretending to check out the rest of the scenery, then casually returned to the table.

"Alright, Don Juan, what was that all about?" Stan asked without mercy.

"Let me partake in my beer and then I'll share my darkest secrets," I responded in mock drunkenness, trying to stall for time. As I raised my mug and started to drink, an image of loveliness appeared through the bottom of the foamed glass. Not trusting my eyes, I quickly put down my beer to find this vision approaching more clearly—and in the flesh.

"Did you want to ask me something?" she inquired innocently.

I wanted to say, "Will you marry me?" but settled for, "Yeah, would you like to dance?"

"Sure." Luckily some angel had popped a quarter into the jukebox for another round of "My Prayer." Closely, I followed her to the dance floor drinking in her scent, a mixture of nutty pine and sunshine. We danced silently at first, me holding her close but not daring to play my pressure games. Her hand was warm and dry and felt just right inside of mine.

"My name is Phil," I finally said. "I work over at the Crystal Arms Hotel—in the dining room."

"Really! You don't look like one of those waiter-types."

"And what exactly is a waiter-type?" I asked, amused.

"Oh, you know." She cocked her head to one side. "Sort of grubby—out to get you," she added with a big smile.

"That sounds terrible," I responded like a wounded puppy. "Actually, I'm lower than a waiter. I'm only a grubby busboy." We both laughed openly to each other, enjoying my self-deprecation. "We'd better get off of me and on to another subject. I'm sinking real fast," I said with rising hopes. "Tell me about yourself."

"Well," she said slowly, starting to roll her eyes as if digging down deep in deliberation. "My name is Laurie and my husband's name is Lance. We live on Long Island and we sell licorice."

"Aren't you supposed to do that with a bouncing ball?"

"Yes, but I'd rather be dancing with you," she flirted.

"Wouldn't Lance object?" I asked coyly.

"Oh, definitely. He'd probably shoot you," she purred.

Enough. I had to speed up my reconnaissance time. Who knew when one of the camp goons might cut in and end my moment in paradise. "So really, what are you doing up here?"

"Real simple. I'm an overgrown camper at Tiroga—and what they do with you when you're ready for pasture is to convert you into a counselor. That's my fate for the summer," she said innocently, looking up at me.

"Hey, Laur, we gotta make curfew," interrupted a large, tired behemoth topped with a crew-cut. "The guys are waiting outside. Let's go," he added gracelessly as he lumbered awkwardly across the dance floor.

"Coming, Jer," she sighed, then turned to me with a smile to light up the countryside and whispered, "See you around, busboy." Then, guarded by her large watchdog, she quickly retreated into the night.

"So who's the doll?" Stan asked eagerly when I returned to the table.

"Oh, just a vision—nothing more," I whispered into my beer.

# CHAPTER 14

The phone in the Camp Tiroga office rang six times. Finally, Bea Rappaport picked it up. "Camp Tiroga—how can I help you?" she singsonged.

"Good evening, I'd like to speak with Laurie, one of your counselors," my friendly voice intoned.

"Which one? We've got three Lauries on staff."

"Three?" My heart sank, then recovered. "I don't know her last name but she's got to be the best looking of all three. She's blond and—just gorgeous!"

"I'm sorry, but I can't just let a stranger talk to one of my counselors. You don't even know her name and I'm responsible for her safety. Sorry!"

"Wait! I'm a friend," I implored.

"Sorry." Click.....She turned to her husband. "The nerve of that young man, trying to encroach on our Laurie. She's Jack's, and that's that." Hy Rappaport said nothing, just shook his head sadly and left the office.

* * *

"Damn!" I slammed the phone down and retreated to the dining room, automatically picking up a cloth napkin and starting to polish my goblets. Stan ambled over quietly.

"Doesn't look like you had too much luck, lover," he said sympathetically.

"Nah! That place is like a fortress. I don't know how I'm going to get through. She's so damned protected."

"The good ones usually are, buddy."

My focus on the goblet in my hand became a stare. Elimination of water spots seemed for the moment to be the one thing in the world I could control. My concentration was abruptly broken when a door slammed and Joann Miller marched into the dining room. She aimed straight for my station.

"What's up, Joann?" I asked, nonchalantly.

"What's up?" she repeated. "Can't a girl stroll into her own dining room without something being up?"

"Guess she can," I answered obediently. "So what's up?"

"Well, actually," she started to whisper slowly, "there's going to be a dance contest in the casino tomorrow night and I thought we'd have a good chance of winning. Can I count on you being there? I think it'd be a lot of fun."

I picked up a goblet and, with one eye closed, peered into it as if the answer to her searing question lay somewhere within it. I then slowly put it down and smiled at her. "Sure, why not?"

* * *

The following morning's air was particularly fresh. It wafted through the Crystal Arms Hotel, causing a quickening in everyone's tempo. Even the older guests were caught up in the exhilaration, eager to get out and inhale the pine scent of nature's finest offerings. Lunch too, went quicker than usual. Sensing the special promise of the day, I decided to spend the extra time by myself. While the rest of the staff went to the lake for a swim, I quietly took out a rowboat and headed toward the opposite shore. My strokes were strong and even as I hit a rhythm, gliding through the cool water which was banded by streaks of brilliant sunlight. I thought of my decision not to go out for crew my freshman year for fear of it affecting my grades. But now, feeling the breeze rush past me as I powered my little craft, I wanted more than ever to go out for the team. The very idea of battling the elements in a sleek scull on a fog shrouded, pre-dawn Spuyten Duyvil, sent a thrill through every muscle in my body....But could I afford the time?

Within twenty minutes I had crossed the lake. I pulled the boat up on the stony shore and looked around. In the four weeks I had been working, I often wondered what was on the other side of the lake. Now, standing there, I could see no evidence of a man-made structure. I looked across at the Crystal Arms Hotel, my hotel, and was surprised at how majestic it appeared, looming up through the pines and reflected upside-down in the still, clear lake. Carol would have described it as "pretty as a picture." I cringed at the thought but was amused that Carol entered my mind at all. I didn't want to think about her. I only wanted to think about Laurie, the elusive one of three counselors with her name-sake at Camp Tiroga. I wandered up an incline until I came to a flat open grassy area dominated by a huge oak tree. Standing next to it, I took in the whole panoramic view of the lake. "It really is beautiful," I thought. "If this place reminds old Mr. Borensweig of Switzerland, I've got some traveling to do once this rat race is over." But right now, I was standing alone, painfully alone in a most exquisite site meant to be shared with the one you love. I closed my eyes and tried to recall the smell of Laurie's hair. The pines responded. The breeze responded. But Laurie was not to be conjured up.

I rowed back across the lake slowly, savoring my solitude. Off in the distance I could see my buddies fooling around on the raft. Not in the mood for horseplay, I tried to detour around them as quietly as possible. But a buxom figure tanning herself on the raft called to me. "Is that you, Phil?" It was Joann.

"I think so," I yelled back flatly.

"Great! I have to get back right away and I don't want to get wet. Could you be a dream and take me in?"

The guys had stopped shoving each other around and were looking at me. Danny broke the silence. "Be a dream, Phil!"

Myron Smith echoed, "Yeah, be a dream, Phil. You know how!" Then they all laughed mercilessly as Joann climbed into the boat with a smug smile on her broad, smooth face.

"You really know how to do it," I scolded, as soon as we were out of earshot. I was now rowing as fast as I could.

"Well, you are a dream," she defended innocently.

"It's more like a nightmare you just created," I said angrily, trying to ignore her flirtation. "These guys will never let go of this one."

"Don't worry, I'll protect you," she smiled sweetly—then added, "Don't forget about the dance contest tonight."

# CHAPTER 15

"Taps" crackled through the P.A. system as the girls of Bunk 9 scrambled to their cots. They knew that the last one under the covers would also be the lucky one to clean the latrine the next day. "I'm in," yelled one little girl. "Say goodnight to me first, Laurie." Methodically, their favorite counselor tucked in and kissed each girl, then announced that she was leaving camp for the evening and that she'd better not hear from the O.D.s that her girls misbehaved. She then threw a sweater over her shoulders and joined her friends waiting outside the cabin.

"You know, once 'Taps' is sounded, you're off," began an annoyed Jack Rappaport. "You don't have to spend the whole night telling bedtime stories to those brats."

"Take it easy, Jack," Laurie said, shaking her head unbelievingly. "These are your kids, too. I can't see how you're going to take over this camp one day with that attitude. Besides, it's still early."

"Where we goin' tonight?" asked a red-faced, prematurely balding Izzy.

"I'm getting tired of Poppy's," chimed in Barb, a short, curly-haired sophomore with a permanent frown.

"Okay, let's go exploring," Laurie offered cheerfully as the counselors worked their way to the parking lot. "There's a hotel on the other side of town where we've never been. It might be fun. I think it's called the Crystal Arms. Let's try it."

"I'm game," said the fifth member of the group—a huge hunk of humanity named Jerry, who, but for a slight heart condition, would have been the dream of any college football line coach. Squeezing into Barb's two-tone Chevy Bel-Aire convertible, a recent gift from her father on her nineteenth birthday, the Tiroga contingency then headed down the gravel road toward uncharted territory.

\* \* \*

The casino was filled and alive with music when they arrived. A dance contest was in progress with two couples left on the floor. The mambo beat stopped suddenly as Al Diamond marched to the center of the spotlight. With cigar in one hand, mike in the other, he gestured to the crowd to applaud the surviving dancers. "Ladies and gentlemen," he began, "we have two fabulous couples here—our own Joann Miller with Phil Dechter from our hotel staff representing the younger generation, and Mr. and Mrs. Marcel Hauser, newcomers to the Crystal Arms this year, who hail from Rego Park, Queens. They're going to face off in the final round in a true test of smoothness and elegance. Who will win the bottle of champagne? Ladies and gentlemen, the Crystal Arms orchestra presents you with…. the Tango!! Couples, please…"

"Can you do this?" Joann whispered to me in a panic.

"The last time I tried was with my mother—at my Bar Mitzvah."

"Oh, no," she sighed as we watched the Hausers glide across the floor as a single graceful entity. They looked like a seasoned skating pair, each knowing by instinct the next subtle move of the other. He was a tall, wiry man with sharp, dark aquiline features and a receding hairline. His wife was petite, yet with large, pale blue sensuous eyes. She would be considered cute, if it weren't for the solemnity of her bearing. Both danced with stark determination.

"We'd better give it a try. The whole world is watching," I muttered philosophically. "Hey, you only die twice." And try we did, but were no match for our experienced and mysterious-looking competitors. The band mercifully ended "Beguin the Beguin" before its time. Then the master of ceremonies presented the Hausers with the champagne,…and an awkward hug. The pair bowed shyly and Mr. Hauser whispered a strongly accented "Zank you." Everyone applauded and soon the dance floor was full.

Joann Miller was furious. She pulled Al Diamond to the side and accused him of a set-up. "Listen, doll," he implored, "your mom wants the paying guests back. You understand that."

I was embarrassed by this confrontation and slinked off in the direction of the bar. Halfway there, I felt a gentle tap on my shoulder. Before I turned, a familiar nutty pine aroma reached my senses and my heart took flight. Yes, it was Laurie.

"You're a better dancer than I thought," she began, looking impressed. "Nice place you've got here."

"How'd you get here?" I asked dumbly. "I mean, how come you're here?"

"My friends and I were looking for a new place to explore—and I remembered the name of your hotel. So we're here. Are you angry that I came?" she asked coyly. Angry! I couldn't find the words to tell her I was thrilled.

"Great! I mean, I'm really glad you came. Do you want to dance?"

"I can't tango."

"Neither can I. Didn't it show?" We laughed but did not lose eye contact.

Laurie felt comfortable and warm in my arms just like the first time I held her. I wanted to close my eyes, if but for a second, just to capture this moment like the shutter of a camera, recording it for all time. "You know," I began softly, "I tried to call you at camp but I didn't know your last name and the woman at the other end wasn't helpful at all. She just cut me off."

"That figures.... But it was real sweet of you to try." She paused as if in deep thought. "I want it to be much easier for you the next time. You just ask for Laurie F. Stillman.... I'm the only one of those around," she added with a broad smile.

# CHAPTER 16

A package arrived for Miss Shana Schectman just as I stopped by the office to mail a letter to my parents. Since I hadn't as yet met Sam's family but was curious to do so, I volunteered to deliver the gift-wrapped box myself. It would be the first time that I would venture down the wooded path to the cottages generally reserved for the married help.

The scene was quaint and very camp-like. The cottages were more like cabins, being lined up on each side of the road. The Schectmans occupied the last one, furthest into the woods. As I approached, I heard giggling coming from behind the building. I walked more softly now, edging my way quietly around the corner so I could steal a glimpse of their lives before formal introductions could be made. I saw a little girl in a frilled pink party dress holding hands and dancing in a circle with a stooped sixty-ish man wearing dark trousers and a white short-sleeved shirt. The only music was their own laughter augmented by the rhythmic clapping coming from a heavy-set woman sitting on the porch, whose pale gray eyes beamed with delight, lending a glow of beauty to her round peasant face. I grinned guiltily as I absorbed this picture from my voyeur's position. The image seemed to be from an earlier time, in another place, perhaps best captured in a sepia-toned freeze frame. Though fascinated, I felt embarrassed that I should witness such an intimate, albeit innocent, picture of Sam's life. I quickly retreated to the front door and knocked loudly. After a few moments, I called out Sam's name.

"Coming, coming, coming, coming," droned Sam's voice as he approached the door. When he saw me, he chirped, "Don't tell me everyone is already sitting at the tables, fork in hand, waiting to be fed."

"No, nothing like that," I responded. "A package came for your daughter and I thought I'd bring it over."

"Smart move, boychik. You can smell a birthday celebration a mile away. Come in and join the party. The invitation must have gotten lost in the mail." I followed Sam through the simple cabin right to the back porch. "Shanaleh! Come here! My Philly brought you a present." Shana inched over, all eyes and blond curls.

"Happy birthday, Shana," I began carefully. "This present is not from me. I just brought it over."

"I told you he was a joker, Shana. Of course it's from him," Sam insisted. "Open it, already."

The little girl attacked the box and in seconds extracted a white dress almost identical to the one she was wearing. She held it out over herself, smiled brightly, then curtsied politely. "Thank you, Mr. Phil," she whispered.

"There must be a card inside," I protested, looking to Esther for assistance, as well as an introduction.

"My lovely wife Esther doesn't speak English, but I know she's pleased to meet you," Sam said. "She knows all about you."

I smiled at her awkwardly, then looked around searching for subject matter. "It's really very nice back here—very quiet and peaceful." Then, turning to Shana, I asked, "Are you having a nice summer?"

"Oh, yes," she perked. "Daddy plays with me all the time."

"You're a very lucky girl, Shana. Your Daddy is a very special man and I like him very much."

Sam coughed as he lit a cigarette. "See what you have to say when you're outnumbered three to one?"

"I've really got to go now." I said. Then turning to Esther, I enunciated very slowly, "It was very nice to meet you," as if the clarity of my voice would help her understand the language. She got up from her rocker and, imitating her daughter's earlier gesture, curtsied to her guest.

In my retreat, I found myself walking in the opposite direction, further into the woods. And to my surprise I found a path which I figured must circle back to the hotel proper. Tall, dense pine trees were everywhere, providing deep shade over the bed of fallen needles below. I made my way along the meandering trail, enjoying the tranquility of yet another serendipitous jaunt. Suddenly, I heard crunching coming the other way—towards me. A lean figure with a walking stick appeared. It was Marcel Hauser. Both of us being equally surprised, greeted one another.

"Hi, Mr. Hauser. I didn't expect to bump into you out here."

"Likewise," he nodded. "It is a little less stuffy here than the casino, yes?"

"You can say that again. By the way, you and your wife really are a handsome couple on the dance floor. Congratulations, again."

"Oh, zank you," he nodded again. "You and your partner deserved to win, too. We should have shared the champagne."

"Oh, no! You won, fair and square. Hey, that's a real nice staff. Did you carve it yourself?"

"Oh, yes. Have a look." He was eager to share his handiwork.

I instinctively ran my hand slowly over the full length of its shaft, pausing at each notched carving. "It's amazing. Did you do it here?"

"Yes. It is so nice to walk in the woods here that I thought I would make a stick to keep me company. I didn't think I would find anyone else doing the same thing."

"Well, I usually don't have the time, but I wish I did. I was just down the road visiting my waiter and his family. They stay in one of the cottages."

"I know. I've seen them on my many walks. He plays with his daughter all the time. It's a pleasure to watch."

"I agree," I enthused. "Do you have any kids yourself? I'll bet they're real cute."

Hauser hesitated for a long time, then said flatly, "No, we have no children."

"I'm sorry." I was very sorry I opened my mouth.

"Don't be sorry. It's not your fault. It is the fault of the times."

"What do you mean, if I may ask," I asked more carefully.

"Come, let us sit." Hauser pointed to a large nearby rock.

I followed, intrigued by this mild, yet mysterious man who, not eighteen hours earlier, had been my adversary in the dance contest. Hauser looked at me a long time, then slowly, almost painfully, emitted, "You are Jewish, no?" I nodded. "You know, you are a very lucky young man—and America is a very great country." I said nothing, eagerly waiting for the follow-up. "You are about the same age I was when Hitler took over Czechoslovakia. I was at the university in Prague, full of hope and with great ambition to be a doctor. My father was a doctor and was looking forward to having me join him. It was a wonderful time. Then it all changed in 1938. I had to leave school. My father was not permitted to practice medicine. Then," he paused with a strange smile, "things really got bad. You asked me a simple question about children, and I will tell you—but with a little background, because you should know. I don't know you but I think you're a smart young man and probably with a bright future. But you must understand the past.

"For me, the future ended in 1938. Almost overnight, what we knew as Jewish society stopped being. The Nazis broke up families. I, with my two younger sisters were sent to a camp at Dachau with many other young people. I never saw my parents again." He paused, gently fingering his

95

carved walking stick. I felt his deep penetrating eyes searching my own for some recognition. I nodded, prodding Hauser on. "I was among the oldest of the youths at the camp. We did not know why we were there, yet the younger ones would look to us for answers. We would make up stories just to keep up hope among the children and sometimes I myself would even believe what I told them. But after several months it was difficult to hide the fact that the future looked black. Many children were getting sick. Others were sent away and rumors were growing that those sent away were going to their deaths. I was searching desperately for something to believe in. Then I met a delicate and frail little girl of fifteen with large, sad blue eyes—my wife, Tina. We fell in love, but in the middle of a world of hate and fear. Together we watched children die all around us and we vowed that if we should survive, we could never bring children into this world. Somehow, we did survive—three years there, then in the resistance for the remainder of the war."

"But that was a long time ago," I protested. "Things got a lot better after the war. You're still young enough...."

"Maybe not physically too old for children, but after what we saw, we know what human nature is capable of—and we don't trust it. We have each other and that is our life."

Reluctantly, I asked," What happened to your sisters?"

"Both died the second year. One from typhus; the other...........committed suicide after a guard raped her."

I stared at Hauser, too shocked to say, "I'm sorry."

"So," Hauser said stoically, breaking the silence, "we don't have any children. But the world will go on. Children will be born, some good, some bad. Maybe yours will be the best." He smiled as he got up from the rock.

"I'd like to talk to you some more sometime, if that's all right," I offered.

"Thank you, but maybe not," Hauser said politely, but emphatically.

"As strangers, we can talk. As friends, it becomes more difficult. Besides, my wife and I are leaving in two days. It has been my pleasure and I wish you much luck." He nodded with a smile and walked off, further into the woods.

# CHAPTER 17

I didn't mind the long walk through town and up the steep gravel and dirt road at the other end. I knew where I was going and more importantly, why. "Just follow the rustic white directional signs to Camp Tiroga and you'll be there," she said. Then I saw the actual gate and my heart started to pound. A bright moon gave the deep lush front lawn a sea-like glimmer, setting off the little white cabins in the distance like just so many tiny "Monopoly" houses. I looked around but saw no signs of life. She said she would be there at nine. I checked my watch. 9:06. Not too bad. Inhaling a deep breath of country air, I hoped to capture not only that special smell of a Catskill twilight, but also the scent of my reason for being there.

"Hello, there." It was her voice, but from where? I gazed about, puzzled. Then a green apple hit the ground and rolled toward me. Looking up, I saw Laurie standing in the crook of two branches of an old apple tree, eight feet above the ground—laughing. The moonlight played on her bright red sweater, accenting her perfectly formed breasts.

"Hello, yourself," I smiled, tossing the apple back at her.

"Catch me," she yelled, jumping recklessly out of the tree. I broke her fall, holding her tight in my arms, then released her. My eyes fixed on her dark eyebrows.

"You're staring at my family trait," she said.

"What are you talking about?" I asked, slightly flushed.

"My eyebrows. You're looking at my bushy eyebrows. They're awful."

"What do you mean? They're great. They're part of you. They've got character."

"Ah, that word, 'character'—the kiss of death," she said, rolling her eyes. You should see my kid brother. He's got them even worse than me. His friends call him King Kong."

"What do his enemies call him?"

"Sir." We both laughed. Then Laurie took my hand and said, "Let's go down the road a bit. I want to show you my favorite spot."

"You mean you're not going to introduce me to the whole camp?"

"God, no! They'll throw you out and Aunt Bea will have a fit. You don't want to know who she is."

"I think I already know."

Laurie led me down the embankment of the road. We followed a shallow creek until it passed under a small stone bridge about one hundred yards downstream. The water was quiet, yet moved quickly over its bed of glistening, half-exposed, smooth stones. I picked one up and examined it. "When you need a skipping stone, you can never find one. And here's a gold mine."

"Bad metaphor, busboy. I thought you went to college," Laurie teased playfully.

"You're right. We pre-med grubs have no couth. Now you're going to tell me that you're an English major. Right?"

"Of course! Don't you know that good literature is what makes the world go round?"

"That,....and beautiful women." I drew her close and kissed her softly on the lips. Then again.

Laurie looked at me a long time, then whispered, "That was very nice.......This is the place."

"It's delightful. But I have to tell you, I've been wanting to be alone with you for so long that any place would be a favorite spot. It may sound corny but I mean it. I'm really excited about being with you tonight."

"That's sweet. I'm kind of happy about it myself. But you know, we don't know anything about each other."

"You're absolutely right, and we've got to change that right now," I insisted. "Shall we sit in your office and discuss it?"

"Sure, over here by the wall." We tiptoed over the protruding rocks, settled in by the side of the bridge, and nestled together, my arms surrounding her shoulders, my cheek next to hers.

"This is weird," I began. "I feel as if I already know you and whatever I tell you, you already know. Isn't that great?"

"In a way, yes. But you still have to tell me about yourself. It's in the rules," she beamed smugly.

"You know, it's funny—the first time I talked to you, you gave me the '*A*, my name is....' routine, and now you're asking me to do the same—only for real. Aren't we more than just names from places and schools?"

"I think you must have a prison record or some other terrible thing in your past. Why else are you avoiding a simple question?"

"Okay! I'm a nice Jewish kid from Washington Heights grubbing my way through Columbia so I can get into a decent medical school. Just like a lot of other guys. I've got an older sister who wants to be an actress. And I've got a fair tennis game and a terrible crush on you."

"It's a start. A promising one." Laurie kissed me softly.

"If I tell you more, will you kiss me again?"

"Maybe. But don't you want to know anything about me?"

"Of course I do, but let me guess." I took Laurie's hand and studied her palm. "I see here that you live on Park Avenue, your father is a banker, and that you go to Sarah Lawrence. Did I hit anything?" I pleaded.

"Not-a-one. You must think I'm some kind of rebellious rich brat or something. Sorry to disappoint your wishful thinking. Quite honestly, I'm insulted."

"Hey, don't be. It's just that all I see is a gorgeous girl with a lot of class."

"Ooh, I hate that word! Usually, anyone who uses the word 'class', doesn't have any." She stood up, folded her arms and strutted a few steps away, staring at the moon.

"Oh man, now I'm in trouble," I lamented. "Can I at least blame the moon for my poor choice of words?"

"Sure," Laurie said to my surprise, returning to her nestled position. "Now I'll set the record straight so you don't have any more illusions about me."

"Please," I said flatly, lifting her ponytail gently and kissing the back of her neck.

"I happen to live on West End Avenue and go to Hunter College. My father is *not* a banker, but my sixteen year-old brother isn't far from it. He sure has a head for money. He's been playing the stock market since he was thirteen, and has already tripled his Bar Mitzvah money."

"I'm impressed. Maybe he can parlay my meager tips into what I expected to make this summer."

"Are they really bad? How does that whole system work, anyway?" Her eyes widened with interest.

"There's really not much of a system. We get room, board, and $15 a week salary. Then, whatever we get in tips, we get. I was hoping to clear $1500 for the summer, but at the rate I'm going, it doesn't look like I'll make it."

"That's a lot of money for a summer."

"It's what I need. A State scholarship doesn't go very far. I don't know what else there is other than being a counselor, and from what I hear, at best, you can't make half that amount. Besides, I'm not sure I could take a bunk-full of kids for a whole summer."

"Oh, kids are great!" Laurie's eyes lit up. "I love them and I want to teach them when I get out of school. Those cute, curious, moldable little people! They're great!"

I smiled in admiration. "Sounds to me like you're pretty committed. It's nice when you don't have second thoughts about what you're doing."

"Does that mean that you do?"

"I always have second thoughts about what I'm doing. It's just me. No! I take that back. Right now, I'm with you and this is exactly where I want to be. Exactly! Absolutely! No question!"

"I like that in a man. It shows good judgment. But tell me about your job."

"Actually, I'm finding it more interesting than I thought. Aside from the disappointing money and the work being pretty intense, I think I might be starting to like it. What's fascinating to me are the people who come up here. I've never seen so many refugees in one place. My own parents are European, but these people are different. Do you know much about the Holocaust?"

"Just a little. My mother's family has been in New York since the 1890's and my other grandparents came over in the twenties, so I don't have any direct family connection. But my father was stationed in Germany during the war and he was in one of those battalions that helped liberate the concentration camps." She started to shake her head slowly. "The stories he would tell us were unbelievable. They found mounds and mounds of bones that used to be people. And the ones that were alive could hardly move, they were so starved. How could people treat other human beings so cruelly? It's hard to imagine. The possibilities of human nature are so scary."

"It's strange that you should say that just now. I was talking to this one guest from the hotel just yesterday who was saying the same thing. You might remember him. He was the one who wiped me out in the dance contest."

"Oh, yes. He and his wife were wonderful. They were such beautiful dancers—but they looked so sad. It seemed so incongruous. Even Jerry, that sweet big oaf, noticed, and he's pretty dense."

"Well—they are sad. Come, let's walk." I pulled Laurie up, then held her hand as we ambled back along the creek. "Mr. Hauser didn't say so, but I think dancing is their one pleasure in life. They were both pretty young when they were caught up in the camps. Somehow they managed to survive together. It must have been absolutely horrible. They seem so bonded now—but they won't have children.........They think the world is too rotten."

Laurie stopped suddenly. "That is so sad. I feel like crying." And a tear did trickle down her cheek.

"You are so beautiful, through and through," I whispered. Then I kissed the tear. The taste of salt mixed with the fragrance of nutty pine— and it was delicious.

# CHAPTER 18

Marty Gould burst through the kitchen doors hoisting a full tray of freshly cleaned water goblets over his head. Stan Simon eyed him suspiciously as he passed his station. Gould continued to the far corner of the dining room where he carefully deposited his tray on a portable stand. Again working alone, he consistently managed to clear out his breakfast guests and set up for lunch while other waiters were still serving second cups of coffee.

"Look at that guy," Stan said to his busboy.

"He's good. What can I tell ya?" replied Bobby Meyers. They watched as Gould locked each drawer of his bussing stand, then promptly left the dining room.

"Nobody else locks up. What's that fucker hiding, anyway?" Stan started again, not expecting an answer.

When the last guest left, Stan walked over to my station, finding me slumped in a chair, very slowly wiping one of my goblets. "You look like shit," he said.

"Thank you," I responded wearily.

"What time did you get in last night?"

"About one."

"And what time did you get back?" he asked with a leer.

"Shut up, asshole. You're not funny."

"Ooh, we're getting serious. I thought they had an 11:30 curfew."

"They do," I said with a sigh, "but it's a long walk back."

"What you need is a set of wheels. *But* they come with a chauffeur who likes female company too. What do you say you ask Miss Wonderful, next time you hike over there, whether she's got a friend for little old me?"

"There's an idea." I perked up, adding, "I'll ask her tonight."

"My, aren't we moving fast," Stan acknowledged with admiration.

"The summer's short," I said flatly.

The main doors opened just then and Ron Miller strolled in, sporting a white tennis sweater draped over his shoulders. Myron Smith turned to Danny and whispered, "I'll bet he never played a game of tennis in his life."

"But he's an ass-man with a shit-load of money. So he can wear whatever the hell he wants," Danny defended.

"Hey, guys," Ron shouted. "Can I have your attention? Why don't you all take a break and come over here for a minute." The thick glasses he wore due to a severe myopic condition were darkly tinted, adding to his aura of 'cool man on the mountain'. He didn't mix with the staff too often but was held in great awe for his reputation as lover and playboy. Even drove a '52 MG Roadster and played a mean jazz piano.

"Listen, fellas," he began when all present were gathered around him, "as most of you know, we've been in friendly competition with the folks at the Matterhorn for quite some time. We're the two largest hotels in town and each of us thinks we're the best. Well—the other night when I was having drinks with Fritzie Baumgarten, he must have had one martini too many. One thing led to another and before you knew it, this clown was challenging us to a softball game. Obviously, he's not aware of the talent we've got here—and who am I to set him straight, right?" He looked around his captive audience through his dark shades. "Anyway, I know what a great staff we've got, and so I took the fool on. It'll be great!

We'll invite the whole town and we've already got the mayor lined up as umpire. It'll be the event of the season." Then, in an exaggerated hushed tone, he added, "My mother doesn't have to know this but I've got a pretty penny riding on this. I know I can count on you boys. I've heard you've had great basketball games going all summer. The transition to softball should be a snap. Anyway, the game's set for the Sunday after next at the Paradise Lake Field. That'll be plenty of time for you guys to practice up. If there's anything you need at all, give me a holler. Remember, the honor of the Crystal Arms Hotel is in your hands. Any questions?"

Murray stood up. "Ron, are you going to join us?"

"With these eyes? Are you kidding? This spaz is going to do more good working the crowd. Anything else?"

"Yeah," Myron Smith responded. "What happens if we lose?"

Ron Miller laughed. "Don't even think about it. By the way, just to keep things flowing—Stan old boy, why don't you captain the team. Keep me posted. I should be here all week. That's it!" As he moved to exit, he threw up his hands and exclaimed, "This is going to be great!" The doors closed behind him. Then, not a sound.

"Shit!" Stan finally broke the silence.

"I thought I signed on to wait tables and just maybe make a few bucks," lamented Sid.

"Now we've got to 'win one for the Gipper'," Danny added.

"…'one for the Gambler' is more like it," quipped Bobby.

"I heard he got thrown out of two colleges for gambling," offered Myron Smith.

"If history is any guide, his 'pretty penny' bet could be anywhere up to five grand," Murray said knowingly.

"Should we tell his Mommy?" Danny asked slyly.

"No way! Anyway you look at it, we're stuck—and we'd better win. And I've got to deliver you guys or he'll have my ass. Shit!" Stan got up and started to pace, then said earnestly, "I have nothing against rich guys. I like Ron. He's a fun guy. But there's one thing that separates them from the rest of us. They've got a safety net. They can take chances, gamble, whatever. They know they'll land on their feet. What they fail to understand is that the rest of us shlubs *have* to succeed. We don't have a choice. They just don't understand that.......And we're gonna need you too, Gould."

"What about me?" Sam asked innocently. Does old man's soccer count for anything?"

"You're our secret weapon, Sam," Stan offered diplomatically. "You're going to give us all the moral support we need."

"God help us all," Sam said, benching twice toward the eastern wall.

"Hey, what's Ron gonna do, fire us all if we lose?" Danny started optimistically. "Let's have a good time. We'll hold our own. It would've been nice if Tommy boy were still around, but what the hell. Let's give it our best shot."

"Danny's used to holding his own. He does it all the time," Myron smirked.

"Okay, okay. Let's not get off the subject," the new captain asserted. "Anybody's who's got any equipment —show up on the back lawn after lunch. We'll throw the ball around."

The group started to break up when Joann Miller came in and walked over to my station. She slyly informed me that a young lady was here to see me and was waiting on the front porch. The owner's daughter had a funny smile on her face and did not seem annoyed—something that surprised me. I looked at Stan, puzzled, and said, "It can't be her,"—then dashed out.

The porch was empty except for one creaky wood rocker facing away from my approach. I advanced quietly, then tip-toed around to discover my mystery guest. "Lisa!" I exclaimed.

"Surprise!" she returned, jumping up to hug her kid brother.

"What are you doing here? You look great!" I picked her up and gave her a twirl. "Did Mom send you up to check on me?"

"No, silly Philly. I've got better things to do."

"Don't let anybody hear you call me that," I warned, playfully.

"Don't worry. It'll remain our dark family secret."

"Where'd you get that floppy sun-hat? It's very *theatrical*."

"Oh, it's a little something I picked up in the Village. Got to keep up with the Bernhardts, you know."

"So what brings you here, pray tell?"

"Well, I just happen to be in the neighborhood," she announced proudly. "Remember all those summer stock auditions I did last May? Well, one paid off and it's just down the road in Holly Falls. It's a major part, too. How does 'The Fourposter' sound to you?"

"Fabulous! I guess I'm going to have to come and see you."

"You're darn right. Think you can scrape up a date?"

"I think I might," I answered coyly.

"Wouldn't be the owner's daughter, would it? She seemed mighty interested in you when I came to the front desk."

"Yeah, I know. That's a little bit of a problem. But, no. Something else might just be developing. Let's leave it at that."

"Come on! Don't be so cryptic. I'm your big sister, remember?"

"You know I'm superstitious. I don't want to blow this. It's too good. Let's see how it goes. How long will you be playing?"

"We're opening at the Playhouse this week-end and if we don't fold in two days, we should last four weeks."

"Great, but don't expect me for at least a week. Hey, I'm really excited for you—and proud. My sister is a star!"

"Don't hand out the Oscars just yet. This is my first big break. By the way, there should be some flyers floating around town promoting the play. If you see one, don't think there's a spelling error. My name is 'Lisa Ann Decker'."

Wide-eyed, I looked at her in silence, then slowly said, "Holy shit! You're really thinking big-time. How do Mom and Pop feel about that?"

"They understand. In fact, I was surprised at how accepting they were. They know that a little Jewish girl from Washington Heights needs all the help she can get."

I pondered that for a moment. "Are you so sure? If you've got it, you've got it. And I think maybe you've got it. Actresses are a dime a dozen. How many are known as good Jewish actresses? You are what you are. Why throw away your whole background? Half of Hollywood is Jewish but you'd never know it. Everyone is trying to hide their Jewishness. That's part of the problem."

"Problem? What problem?"

"Oh,......call it survival of the species. I don't know."

"Am I hearing this from my brother? You never talked like that. What's gotten into you?" she asked, shaking her head.

"It's weird. I don't know any more about the Holocaust than you do. But I've met people up here who were actually in it. They seem to have suffered so much—and lost so much, just for being Jewish. It's got to count for something."

"Maybe..... Listen—the sun is shining and I only have a couple of hours. I came over to surprise you and have some laughs. We'll talk about this some other time."

"You're right." I looked around warily, then, with great delight, observed, "Hey, nobody's around and I see two thrones over there.... Shall we?"

"Of course," she responded. "Let's do it." Brother and sister walked hand in hand to the end of the porch where we deposited ourselves very stiffly into two side-by-side high-backed wooden chairs with armrests.

"Is the court assembled, my lady," I inquired in a mock British accent, grasping the armrests like a sphinx in the desert.

"Indubitably, my sire," she answered haughtily.

"Then let us begin. How are the subjects behaving?"

"In check, my lordship, but a bit restless. It seems they are not happy with the crumbs we gave them last week."

"Well, in that case, a flogging is definitely in order. Call the guards!"

"Cool it, Phil. I hear someone coming," Lisa interrupted. I turned to see a hunched figure approaching, newspaper in hand and with a cigarette dangling from his mouth.

"Sam," I called out. "Come over here and meet my sister."

"Your sister?" Sam responded. "What a pleasant surprise. I am honored to meet you." He took her hand and bowed politely. "I hope you're not here to take him away. He's a good worker and I like him. Besides, he has a beautiful sister."

"You're a charming man, Sam. Thank you very much," she beamed. "I'm Lisa."

"Ah, with a beautiful name to match. Pardon me. I just came outside for a little fresh air and to read about the outside world. Maybe there's some news besides Eisenhower's golf game. I'll leave you two alone." He bowed again and retreated in the opposite direction.

"What a nice old man," Lisa confided.

"The ultimate mensch," I confirmed. "He's one of those guys who carries the world on his back and doesn't flinch. As bent over as he is, he's stronger than all of us."

# CHAPTER 19

The black Ford rumbled up the dirt road, spitting gravel in all directions. Its headlights strained to penetrate the evening fog, searching for two counselors at the end of the road. The driver turned nervously to his companion, "I'm telling you, Phil, if she's a dog, we're not going to Poppy's. I've got a reputation to keep up."

"Don't worry, Stan. She won't be a dog. Laurie said she was real nice. And no, I did not ask if Barb goes down. You're a big boy and you'd better behave yourself—not the way you screwed me over at the Garlands. Because this time, I *do* care. Comprende?"

"You're on, buddy! Hey, this really is a hike. You sure have the hots for this babe. But I've got to hand it to you, though. She's a real score."

"Yup."

The familiar camp gate came into view and as promised, the girls were waiting. Their silhouettes were sharp and very different. Laurie was not tall but seemed to loom over her diminutive, stick-built friend, whose closely cropped curly hair gave her a poodle-like, pixie aura. Laurie wore her hair loose. Stan and I got out of the car and introductions were made.

"It looks so foggy tonight," Laurie began. "Shouldn't we stay close to home—maybe just go to Poppy's?"

"Nah! It's not bad. I can drive through anything," Stan quickly insisted. "Let's be adventurous. I heard there's a track for harness racing over in Mountaindale. It could be a lot of fun."

"That's twenty miles away," I argued.

"So what! I'm doing the driving. Let's go." The four of us piled into the Simobile and gravel started to fly.

"So where do you go to school, Stan?" Barb started.

"N.Y.U. What about you?"

"Boston College. I just love the Boston area. There's so much going on," she gushed. "What's your major?"

"Psych."

"Me, too," she squealed. "Isn't that exciting?"

"Yup. It's a small world," Stan said without enthusiasm. Silence.

Laurie piped up from the back seat, "I've never been to the track. What's it like?"

"Don't ask me," I said, taking her warm hand in mine. "I've never been there either."

"Looks like it's up to you to enlighten us, Stan," Barb perked.

"Well, folks, I'm no old-time track-rat. I've only been to the Aqueduct, and only twice at that. What I can tell you is that it's exciting. Everybody's got money riding on these poor horses, mostly only $2 a shot. But they're all screaming their heads off—and it's contagious. The adrenalin just flows with the manure."

"Such poetry!" I interjected. "Doesn't Stan have a special way with words, ladies?"

"There is a certain imagery there," Laurie went along.

"Okay, okay, go ahead and trash me," Stan said. "But let me set the ground rules right now. It's easy to blow a whole lot of money, but that's not going to happen to us. Why? Because Phil and I don't have much to start with. Sorry to be crude, but that's the way it is. We'll all start with a budget of, say $8. That's good for four races. And if anybody wins, we split the wealth and start all over." He then added slyly, "The real fun is watching all the nuts go crazy—and that may include us. Sound okay?"

"But how do we know which horses to pick?" Barb asked.

"Easy. You're wearing a yellow sweater. Pick a jockey who's got gold satins on. A sure winner. Or, if you're not into colors, find a horse's name that reminds you of your grandmother or something. I tell you, it's a real science." Everyone laughed.

"We've got a regular Nathan Detroit here," I said, hoping Stan's sarcasm wasn't too much for Barb. "How about a little music?"

"You're on!" Stan fiddled with the radio dial until he found something he liked. Frank Sinatra was in good voice lamenting about the "wee small hours of the morning." "It's early, Frank," Stan chided. "It's the fog that makes it look so damn late."

"Nice an' easy, Stan. Don't blame Frank. Just keep your eyes on the road," I pleaded. "Maybe Frank wants a little company. What do you think, girls?" Soon, all of us joined in and Sinatra tunes penetrated the night air, but not the fog.

When we finally rolled into the track parking lot, Barb announced her desperate need for a bathroom. Laurie accompanied her, leaving me glaring at Stan. "Why are we here?" I demanded.

"Because she's a mouse," Stan answered defiantly.

"That's not a dog."

"What's the difference?"

I winced, then whined, "Hey, this is going to cost us a fortune."

"I set the limits didn't I?"

"Yeah, real smooth, too," I answered with a roll of my eyes.

When the girls returned we entered the track proper, with the noise of the crowd reaching a crescendo, signaling the final turn of the current race. We rushed toward the rail to catch a glimpse of the excitement. A flurry of color greeted us as the pack of furious little chariots passed by. Between the wheels, the whips, the hoofs and the yelling, the overall sound was deafening—and thrilling. As quickly as the noise had escalated, it now subsided. The race had ended. A few tired looking old men walked away from the rail, tearing ticket stubs. In fact, most of the patrons were little old men. One skinny, toothless codger hobbled over and stared at Laurie. He finally said, "Hey, honey, wanna tip?"

"Sure."

"Don't bet on Ranger. He ain't what he used to be." The black gap between his wrinkled lips remained open, waiting for a reply.

"Thanks, mister. I'll remember that," Laurie said, looking to her companions for support. The old man nodded, then trudged off to a corner where he relieved himself against a concrete wall.

Oblivious to the scene, Barb remarked on the paucity of women. Stan sloughed it off with, "Don't complain. Now you'll be a standout in the crowd."

I picked up a few race forms and handed them out. We novices studied them diligently, concluding that the only thing we really understood was that we had missed the first three races. "Have you found your grandmother yet, Barb," Stan asked.

"No, but the horses do have the neatest names. I think I'll go with 'Old Thunder'."

"Uh, oh. I wouldn't want to be running behind him," Stan chimed.

"What do you mean?"

"Never mind. We haven't heard much from you, Laurie. See any winners in there?"

"I sure would like to see the horses that go with these names—sort of to get the right vibrations. For $2, we're entitled to that, aren't we?"

"She's precious, Phil. She knows the value of a buck. Maybe we can work our way over to the staging area and compare names with faces."

"Won't we miss another race?" asked a concerned Barb.

"So what?" Stan said. "Just so much less money to blow." He proceeded to lead us through the crowd, but then stopped suddenly.

"Hey, Phil, check ticket window #2," he said in a serious tone. "Look who's into the trotters." We both stared incredulously as we watched Marty Gould talking to a man wearing a green Tyrolean hat. "Explains a few things, doesn't it?"

"Who's that?" Barb asked innocently. "He's kind of cute."

"Let's just say he works with us, sort of," I answered.

"He's someone you probably don't want to know," Stan added in a fatherly tone. "Let's keep going."

The horses in the staging area snorted impatiently, yet to their observers, they still appeared majestic in their colorful finery. "Oh, look at that one," ogled Laurie, pointing to a dark chestnut filly with an ultra-marine blue headdress. "She's gorgeous. What's her name? What's her name? Let's see—number eight." She fidgeted with the race form, then exclaimed, "Of course—'Blue Velvet.' What else could her name possibly be? She's the one for me. She's got my $2. I just hope she's not done racing for the night."

"What about you, Phil boy?" Stan asked. "I'm all set with that skinny gray one over there named 'Bad News'."

"Why 'Bad News'?"

"Because I'm a bottom-line kind-a-guy and bad news travels fast."

"Hey, that's good thinking," I countered, "but I'm going to fly with a more upbeat horse, like 'Prince Valiant'. Hi-O, Prince Valiant." Starting to feel giddy, the four of us then ran to the nearest window and placed our bets.

"Nothing's happened and I'm excited already," Laurie announced as we settled into our seats. The next race had all of our chosen steeds running, as well as eight others. Laurie and Barb hung on to us guys, screaming wire to wire. In the end, it was "Old Thunder" placing second, causing Barb to jump up with a girlish squeal. To my surprise, Stan grabbed her and planted a big kiss on her no-longer-poodle-like face.

That moment of euphoria turned out to be the highpoint of the evening's gambling. Our luck went downhill from there. But we loved the color and excitement and, to Stan's satisfaction, our budget was kept. We walked to the parking lot, arm in arm, exhausted from the yelling—but still smiling.

Rather than let up, the fog had thickened, giving the pole lights in the lot an eerie, unfocused glow. We climbed into the car and started the long trek back to Paradise Lake. Laurie and I got very cozy in the back seat, not finding much need for animated conversation. Barb, however, still high from her horse's second place finish, chatted endlessly. And Stan, peering desperately through the windshield, tried to keep his wheels between the elusive white lines.

"You're driving very slow, Stan," Barb observed. "Are you sure we're going to make curfew?"

"Well, darlin', I'll give you a choice. We either crawl through this pea soup and maybe get back,....or we die."

"Easy for you to say. We've got obligations."

"Do you think they'll pin a medal on one of your body parts that they find strewn all over the road after a head-on collision? I can see the newspaper headline now. *'Dedicated counselor dies trying to make curfew'.*"

"Very funny. Remember, it was your idea that we drive this far in the fog," Barb reminded.

"Hey, did you have a good time?" Stan asked.

"Yes, I had a good time," she said emphatically.

"Good. If you want to do it again, you'll simmer down and help me stay on the road."

"Did I hear right?" Laurie piped in from the back. "Did Mr. Tough Guy ask for help?"

"Hey, go back to making out. I'm not talking to you."

"What do you want me to do, Stan?" Barb asked softly.

"Roll down your window and just watch your side of the road. Tell me if we're getting too close to the shoulder."

"Sure," she said, patting his forearm gently. "Just be careful." We limped back to camp and missed curfew by forty-five minutes.

# CHAPTER 20

Paradise Lake Field was a euphemism for a dandelion convention. But the bases and backstop were there. So were the stands—and most important of all on this sunny Sunday, they were filled, even complemented by an array of beach-chairs along the third base line.

The team from the Matterhorn Hotel was in the field, still practicing before the 1:30 game start. The Crystal Arms staff watched from the sidelines, trying to get a clue of what awaited them. Suddenly, Danny yelled out, "Hey, look at the Hornies. They play like a bunch of yodelers!" The team in the field glared back.

"Great!" sighed Murray. "Now we've got a war on our hands—not just a game."

"It's okay. We could use a little firing up," Stan said as he started to clap his hands. Others followed.

"Do you think Ron will let us keep these hats?" Myron Smith asked, curling the beak of his new "C/A" emblemized baseball cap.

"Maybe—but only if we win," Stan answered. "What do you think of these guys?"

"Given our two practice sessions, it's a definite toss-up," an authoritative Sid Goldhammer declared.

Rudi Ostheimer, the town mayor, worked his way along the beach-chairs, shaking hands and waving to familiar as well as totally unfamiliar faces in the stands. Ron Miller, meanwhile, wearing his "C/A" hat, entertained a group of hotel guests in the stands, explaining the rudiments of the game of softball to those uninitiated. The crowd of about two hundred spectators, for the most part, was there out of curiosity. The locals hadn't seen a game played on that field in years and were anxious to see the talents of the young city-slickers from New York. The hotel guests were there mainly at the urging of their hosts who billed the event not only as a battle of the giants, but also, and of even more significance—as a free treat.

At exactly 1:30, the mayor strode out to the pitcher's mound with a bull-horn and addressed the crowd. He praised the two hotels for being so civic-minded as to create such a wonderful community event, bringing together both town folk and guests from far and wide to share in the great American pastime. Looking like an introduction to a prize fight, he bid the two owners come out and join him. Ron Miller and Fritzie Baumgarten shook hands to everyone's applause. Then Rudi flipped a coin and Ron called "tails." Tails it was, and the home team took the field.

On our way out, Stan asked me, "Think the girls will show up?"

"Only if they can convince the camp that this is a legitimate field trip for the kids. Don't hold your breath."

As the first batter came to the plate, Danny, playing shortstop, started his taunt. "Hornies can't hit. Boy, does this guy look horny. He should have stayed on the mountain." The hitter promptly grounded to Gould at third who easily threw him out.

Fritzie Baumgarten, sitting behind home plate with Ron Miller, turned to his companion and complained in his thick German accent, "Tell your boys to stop making fun of the Matterhorn. It's bad for business."

"Right. As soon as they come in from the field," Ron smiled slyly.

After an error at second base, two long fly balls to Stan in centerfield ended the Matterhorn's first ups. As Danny was first to bat for the Crystal

Arms, Ron strode over to the plate and told him to cool the name-calling—but also to keep the heat up.

Owner Baumgarten had outdone his counterpart in outfitting his boys with shirts as well as hats. The famous profile of the Swiss mountain loomed impressively on the chest of each player with "Matterhorn Hotel" scrawled across it. Two points for Fritzie.

Seeing Stan jog over to coach first base, Sam Schectman, wearing his trademark white—on-white shirt, took up his position as designated third base coach. Having absolutely no idea of what he was supposed to do, he immediately started to pace nervously. Having also been asked not to smoke didn't help his sense of belonging. He saw Stan clapping his hands so he started clapping too.

Danny grounded to shortstop, but after a slight bobble, beat the throw to first base. I was up next, conventional wisdom calling for a left-hander to bat second. I promptly hit a double to right field, bringing Danny home with the first run of the day. Sam turned to the stands and raised his arms. The Crystal Arms fans cheered in response. After two caught fly balls, a long triple by Bobby Meyers sent me around third base. Sam, redundantly, waved me home. But that was all the scoring that took place that inning. Meanwhile, Joann Miller and her mother paraded happily along the bottom of the stands, loudly offering free lemonade and assurances that their boys would maintain their lead.

Midway into the second inning, a dozen girls could be seen marching in from the dandelion fields toward the stands. Stan and I looked at each other with satisfaction. Our fans had arrived. Laurie and Barb led their girls quietly to the sidelines where they were joined by their eager hosts.

"It's great that you made it," I beamed.

"It wasn't easy, believe me," Laurie said. "Now you've got to make it worthwhile—and win the bloody game."

"Hey, we're trying. The pressure is on," Stan added.

"Isn't that the guy from the race track?" Barb asked, pointing to Gould on the bench.

"Sure is," Stan frowned. "He's no prince, but he can play ball."

"What's the score?" Barb asked.

"We're up, 2—0."

Laurie turned to her campers and shouted, "Okay, girls, let's do it!" Ten nine-year olds promptly spread out along the third base line and shouted in unison to the crowd, "Crystal Arms! Crystal Arms! Boom, boom, boom! Crystal Arm! Crystal Arms! Score, score, score!" Then the smallest of them stepped forward and did three cartwheels as the others clapped. The team, as well as the crowd, roared its approval. Laurie looked impishly up at me and declared, "It's the best we could do in one rest hour."

"That was just great!" I gushed. Mrs. Miller came over just then and asked what that was all about. "Any team can use a cheering squad," I answered sheepishly with a grin.

"Who needs them? We're winning, aren't we?" an angry Joann burst in with hands on her hips.

"So far, Joann. Just so far," countered Stan in a foreboding voice.

The Matterhorns scored three times in the fourth inning to take the lead, thanks to a bobble and miss-throw by Gould, followed by a triple to right field. As the home team came to bat, Gould complained to Stan that his real position should be left field—that he wasn't comfortable playing the infield. He hit a double that inning, and while not scoring, was rewarded his wish. In the fifth inning, each team scored twice.

Before his team could take the field, Ron Miller hustled over to the bench and quietly addressed his troops. "Hey, listen up, guys. This is only a seven inning affair. We're down by one and don't have much time. Remember what I told you in the dining room." He continued in a more agitated voice, meeting eyeball to eyeball with each player. "There's money riding on this. I want you to turn the juice up." A nervous team left the bench but managed to hold the Matterhorns scoreless. In the bottom of the sixth, it was also the bottom of the batting order for the tray-bearers and bellhops of the Crystal Arms Hotel.

Sam had gotten a little more comfortable with his position by this time, realizing that he was one of the few Miller employees who hadn't as yet made a mistake. He was also slowly learning the basic rules of the game. He yelled to the first batter, "Come on, boychik, you can do it. Hit a homer!" Murray Koenig answered the call with a harmless grounder to the pitcher. This only animated Sam even more. "Come on, Sidney," he screamed. "Hit the ball far. It will make you a better lawyer. The pitcher can't pitch and the umpire can't umpire." Since we were playing slow-pitch softball, there were no called strikes and so there really wasn't much for Rudi Ostheimer to do other than look ceremonious and keep the game going. Yet Sam felt compelled to badger him. "The umpire can't see," he continued.

Finally, the mayor raised both arms halting play, and called out, "Mr. Miller, do you think you can control your non-playing team members?"

"Take it easy, Sam," Ron laughed. "It's only a game." Sam was incensed at the patronization but held his silence.

When the game continued, Sid Goldhammer hit two foul balls, then missed the next pitch, thereby becoming the first strikeout victim of the day. Then, with two out, Danny hit a sharp single over second base, which, after a bobble by the outfielder, he stretched into a double. Now, feeling the full pressure of the moment, I came to the plate and took the first three pitches. The Matterhorns in the field were clammering for an out while my teammates were just making noise. Hoping to settle down, I looked around for encouragement. Sam was quietly staring at the ground, but I found it in Laurie. She didn't say a word—just smiled a smile meant only for me. I hit the next pitch deep down the rightfield line, bringing Danny easily home. Urged on by the crowd, I rounded second base and headed for third. A perfect throw was rifled in from the outfield as I tried to slide in under the tag. A surge of dust rose from the ground, but Rudi was right there. He called me out. Sam jumped in the air and yelled, "You're crazy. He's safe!"

"He's out," Rudi repeated.

"You're blind," Sam railed.

"Get lost," Rudi countered, addressing Sam for the first time.

"No, you get lost!"

I slowly got up from the ground, gradually becoming aware of the silence overcoming the field. All eyes were on the two men as the tension between them mounted with each verbal encounter.

"You get lost!" Rudi continued as the two slowly approached each other. They stared at one another for what seemed to the crowd as a painful forever. Then, to everyone's amazement, rather than come to blows—they embraced. Standing together, with arms locked around each other, they were motionless—except for the tears which flowed generously from each survivor.

Of all the people assembled there that afternoon, I was the only one not bewildered by what was witnessed. I understood. From my close position, I could just barely make out the imprints on each of their forearms as they gripped one another with great intensity. One read "24934," the other, "24935."

After a few moments, the equivalent of thirteen years, they let go of each other. With only a mutual nod to acknowledge what had just happened, they quietly separated. The teams changed positions in the field and Rudi resumed his post behind the pitcher. "Play ball!" he yelled.

The spectators who had already seen more than they bargained for, were hushed as the seventh and last inning began. The score was now tied 5 to 5. The first Matterhorn player to bat popped up weakly to first base but was followed by a sharp single to left field. The next hitter lined a shot over the pitcher's head. Danny lunged and miraculously snared it before crashing to the ground. Joann Miller leaped from her seat with glee, but her joy was short-lived as she saw him limp slowly off the field, holding his elbow. No one could tell if it was broken, but one thing was for sure— he could not continue to play. Stan yelled to his team-mates to switch positions. Myron Smith would come in from the outfield to play shortstop and Sid Goldhammer would leave his semi-useless catcher's post to cover right field. Someone would cover home plate, if necessary, and in the meantime, Joann volunteered to retrieve pitched balls. With two out, the next batter hit a fly ball to right field. Coming in and misjudging it completely, the future lawyer watched the ball sail over his head and bounce playfully among the dandelions. By the time he got the ball back to the infield, runners were secured at second and third base.

"Okay, guys," Stan yelled in from centerfield. "Let's dig in. One more out to go." The next sound was the crack of a bat sending a high fly ball to deep left field. Gould started to back-peddle, following the path of the ball as it arched its way through the glaring sun above. He circled hesitantly, lost it, then heard a thud on the ground just behind him. Retrieving the ball, he fired it into second base, but the damage was done. Both runners had already scored. The next batter popped up to shortstop.

The team was deathly quiet as it came in from the field for its final licks. Turning to Gould, a restrained Stan Simon broke the silent tension, "You should've had it."

"I lost it in the sun."

"You should have had it, anyway."

"I don't hear you complaining to Goldhammer," Gould lashed back.

"Don't bullshit me. You're supposed to be a ballplayer," Stan answered, getting more agitated.

"Cool it, guys," the injured Danny interrupted. "We're only down by two. We still have a chance."

Meanwhile, on another part of the field, Fritzie Baumgarten, enjoying a cold drink, turned to his fellow hotel owner and asked smugly, "Are you finding the game exciting enough for your taste?"

"We're not done yet, Fritzie," Ron Miller answered without expression.

"Just remember, I want cash, not your crummy surplus foodstuffs." Then, wiping his sweaty forehead, Fritzie Baumgarten placed his green Tyrolean hat over his bald pate and returned his attention to the game.

Bobby Meyers was the first to step up to the plate. I glanced over to Laurie. To my surprise, I saw her mobilizing her girls for another cheer.

"Crystal Arms, Crystal Arms, boom, boom, boom! Crystal Arms, Crystal Arms, score, score, score! "It gave the Miller guests something to clap for and also broke the ice for the team on the bench.

I stood up and shouted, "Come on, Bobby, let's get something started."

Sam, reticent since his outburst, seemed to have found a new vigor and chimed in, "Bobby boy, if you get a hit I'll do your goblets tonight."

Bobby smiled and yelled back, "You're on, buddy," then put all his concentration on the ball. After letting the first three pitches go by, he hit a screaming single through second base. A collective cheer erupted from the bench, then grew suddenly still as Marty Gould came to bat. He looked menacing at the plate, big and dark and brooding. He sent the first pitch deep down the left field line—foul. Same for the next pitch.

Finally, a word of encouragement from the bench. "Straighten her out, Gould," Stan yelled. But the next swing brought a towering fly ball to left field, also foul—but high enough for the fielder to camp under it and bring it in. Mickey, the bellhop, was next to bat. He grounded to the third baseman who, seeing an opportunity for a game-ending double-play, flipped the ball to second base for out number two. Bobby Meyers, however, came crashing into the second baseman, sending both of them sprawling—and preventing the relay to first. As Bobby got up from the ground with a smirk firmly planted on his besmudged face, he found himself being pushed back down by the second baseman, who had taken umbrage to his rough treatment. Immediately, there were fifteen players from both teams squaring off at second base, ready to start World War III.

Rudi Ostheimer threw both hands up in the air as if Moses himself were ready to cast the sacred tablets to the earth. He yelled to both sides, "Please—if you must fight, fight for something worthwhile, not a stupid baseball game. Please, let us have peace." There was urgency in his voice, beyond the call of a small town mayor asking for civility. The players returned to their positions and Myron Smith stepped to the plate.

Seeing that Stan was next to bat, the pitcher threw nothing close to the plate, hoping Myron would swing at a bad pitch. After the fifth toss, frustration set in and Myron swung at a high and outside pitch, drilling it to right field for a single. Arriving at first base, he received a big hug from Joann Miller, then called out to third base, "Hey, Sam, will you do my goblets too?"

His waiter, Murray, cut him off, "No he won't, but if you don't shut up, I'll kick your ass."

Quiet set in again as Stan stepped up to home plate. Two out, two men on base, and two runs behind. He took several practice cuts with two bats, trying to intimidate the pitcher as well as shore himself up. He knew Ron Miller was a reasonable person and shouldn't hold his appointed captain personally responsible for losing the game. Yet if he were to lose big in his bet with Fritzie Baumgarten, it would be difficult to imagine him other than vindictive. Stan tossed aside the lighter of the two bats and dug in. It was now all or nothing. He would wait for the perfect pitch. When it came, he swung with all his weight shifting to his front foot, sending the ball soaring over the centerfielder's head. The two base runners didn't need coaxing as they scampered in to tie the score. Now only Stan was on the base path, racing toward home to beat the throw. He slid in, face first, taking the poor catcher for a surprise joy ride through the dust. Safe! The Crystal Arms Hotel wins, 8-7.

It was standing room only in the stands as incredulous spectators cheered their approval for what they had just witnessed. Aged refugees hugged straight-haired townie teen-agers, while on the field, a jubilant mound of waiters and busboys piled up on a prostrate Stan Simon. It was difficult to distinguish body from body and joy from relief.

As they unscrambled, a happy Bobby Meyers asked Sam, "Will you really do my goblets?"

"It will be my pleasure, Bobby boy, my true pleasure," Sam beamed.

Only Ron Miller and Fritzie Baumgarten remained motionless in their seats. In a dry, business-like tone, a demure Mr. Miller remarked, "You did insist on a cash transaction, did you not?"

# CHAPTER 21

For a full twenty-four hours after the game Stan Simon was treated like a hero at the Crystal Arms Hotel. Despite his natural cynicism, he felt good enough about his performance and the way things turned out that he offered me the use of his car, should I choose to visit Camp Tiroga alone. I immediately took him up on his generosity, thinking I would like to take Laurie to my sister's play in Holly Falls.

Three days later, embedded in Stan's black Ford, Laurie and I cruised east on Route 21. A slight breeze passed through the open windows as I stole a glimpse her way. Her bright eyes sparkled in the early twilight as a few stray hairs danced on her smooth tanned neck. I wanted to stop the car and kiss that warm tender spot, but restrained myself.

"I'm real curious to see my sister act," I said. "I haven't seen her on stage since she was in high school."

"It must be great to have an older sister."

"It must be great to have a younger brother," I countered. We both laughed.

"Actually, you seem very proud of her," Laurie said.

"I am. We're very close, but we don't see much of each other. Does that sound strange?"

"Not really. I can understand that." Laurie thought a moment, then continued. "I love my brother but I see so much of him that I don't really have an opportunity to appreciate him. Does that sound weird?"

"Either we're both weird or we're both very normal. You look great!"

"Thanks,....I love your nonsequiturs."

"Anytime," I said, flashing a smile. I then put my free hand on hers and drove on in silence.

We arrived at the playhouse with just ten minutes to spare before curtain time. The building was a converted barn, typical of many summer stock theaters with its aging vertical planks stained a deep red. In addition to a large hand-painted sign promoting "The Fourposter," there was a typewritten sheet tacked next to the entrance door announcing the performers and their roles. Heading the list was Lisa Ann Decker. I had forgotten about the name change and, as I stared at the piece of paper, was filled with both pride and embarrassment. I explained to Laurie that Lisa had made the change to enhance her career.

She looked me straight in the eye and asked, "But you don't like it, do you?"

"No." Then looking at the ground, "I don't know who Lisa Ann Decker is."

"Come, let's go find out," she said cheerfully.

The interior of the playhouse was Spartan, yet friendly, with huge dark wooden trusses spanning the space. Loose, mismatched chairs filled the orchestra which itself, was only half filled with people. I guessed that only about one hundred onlookers would share my view of my sister that evening. Laurie and I took our seats and quietly scanned the audience.

"When my brother and I find ourselves waiting in a crowd, we like to speculate about the lives of the people around us," Laurie whispered. "It's so much fun—and it passes the time."

I didn't dare divulge the secret game of "King and Queen" that I shared with Lisa for moments like this. Laurie would make fun of me. Or, at any rate, I wasn't ready yet. "Okay, let's find an interesting couple," I said.

"Hey, look at those two farmers in the first row," Laurie glowed.

"At least they're wearing clean overalls."

"I'll bet their wives sent them to the theater so they could bake their apple pies in peace."

"Would you listen to us? We sound like a couple of condescending city-slickers," I admonished. "Those guys are probably local bankers and own the town."

"Yeah, you're probably right," she agreed. "But do you think the tall bearded one's pipe is lit? We're just speculating now, remember."

"It damn well better not be. This barn will go up in flames in a minute." The lights then dimmed and the curtain rose.

Two and a half hours later the final curtain fell to the enthusiastic applause of the few assembled. "What did you think?" I asked eagerly.

"I thought she was great! More importantly, what did you think?"

"I think she aged too fast. I don't like to see her looking old."

"How infantile! I don't believe you said that," Laurie scolded, shaking her head. "It's part of the script. Blame the make-up man if you like. It's the acting that counts and she was great."

"You're right, she was good. I guess I'm still having a hard time believing she's my sister. *Lisa Ann Decker*. Huh."

"I'd love to meet her."

"That's why you're here. I mean,.... sure. Let's go."

We worked our way through the loose chairs to the backstage. Lisa was already holding a glass of red wine and engaged in animated conversation with the tall, overalled gentleman holding his pipe. Spotting her brother, she squealed, "Phil, Phil," and ran over with outstretched arms. A little wine spilled on my sports jacket as I hugged her back, but that was alright. I was delighted that the production's star should fawn on me.

"You were great," I gushed. "Can you take off that gray wig now? I want you to meet my date, Laurie."

"Hi!" she said ignoring my request, then dragged us both over to the bearded "farmer," exclaiming, "You have to meet my stage manager..... Mitch, my kid brother finally showed up. This is Phil and his girlfriend, Laurie.... This is my good friend, Mitch Gustafson."

Hi's and handshakes were exchanged. Then Laurie said, "Lisa, you were just fabulous. How can you go out there night after night and spill your guts out like that?"

"Trade secret," Lisa laughed.

"Actually," Mitch Gustafson interjected, "it's all in the props." Still puffing deliberately on his unlit pipe, he added, "Let me show you around the backstage area." He then took Laurie by the arm, leaving brother and sister alone.

"I know you're high as a kite," I began, "but you sure take a lot for granted."

"What do you mean?"

"I never said Laurie was my girlfriend."

"So what? It's obvious you want her to be and I don't blame you. She's cute as hell."

"That's not the point. It's still early and I don't want to scare her off."

"Ooh, this is serious."

"By the way," I said, "how good a friend is this Mitch? He looks old enough to be your father."

"Oh, it's just the beard that makes him look older. He's actually only thirty-four. And he's brilliant. Knows everything about the theater."

"How come the stage manager is watching the show from the first row?"

"My, you're observant, little brother. After a week and a half of the play's running, he just felt confident enough to want to see what the play looked like from the audience....... You know," a testiness developing in her voice, "I don't like your line of questioning. I thought you were coming here to see me act and to share in whatever glory I can muster in this rat race. Instead, you're criticizing every move I make. I'll see whoever I damn well want to see. Old, young, black or white. Jewish or not Jewish. I'm twenty-three and don't need my Ivy League, goody-two-shoes brother to tell me how to lead my life. Understood?"

"Whoa! Talk about over-reacting," I said, raising both hands in the air defensively. "Did I say anything about him not being Jewish?"

"No, but you were thinking it," she said in a lowered voice.

"Maybe....... Hey, I just want everything to work out right. For you, for me, for everyone.... I'm sorry."

"Well, you can't script your life, sonny boy. It just doesn't work that way."

"Spoken like a true actress," I said, smiling in my most conciliatory tone.

"Give me another hug, silly Philly," Lisa said with both arms open. "Laurie really is a doll."

Laurie and Mitch returned to their partners. "This place is amazing, Phil," Laurie exuded. "Mitch says he bought the barn five years ago and made the conversion almost single-handedly."

"I'm impressed," I responded. "You did a great job."

"Thank you," Mitch nodded, taking Lisa's hand in his.

"Was tonight a typical turnout? I mean.... do you consider this a successful run?"

"Don't start, Phil," Lisa said angrily.

"Ah, you noticed a few empty seats, did you?" a glint of emotion finally coming from Mitch as he addressed me. "Actually, we do get a few more patrons on the week-end. But if you're asking if we're making any money, I'd have to say, 'Probably not.' Summer stock is a labor of love. If I wanted to make money, I'd have shaved my beard and become a stock broker."

"This is a way of life," Lisa declared, glaring at me and squeezing Mitch's hand.

Looking around awkwardly, I asked, "Is there a place we can go and talk, maybe to get something to drink?"

"There's nothing for miles, but you can come to our cabin for a cup of coffee," Lisa offered.

Staring at the wood floor, I did not respond. But Laurie said, "I'm afraid we really can't. Time just flew by and I've got a curfew to meet. Sorry to be the pooper. It really would have been fun. But it's been great to meet you both."

"She's right. We do have to go," I said. "Till we meet again.... on Broadway."

"That'll be the day," Lisa responded, rolling her eyeballs.

"Don't sell yourself short, my sweet. You have a lot of talent," Mitch said.

"I'll say," Laurie added. "I'm sure you'll be there soon."

"I like this one," Lisa said, giving Laurie a hug. "With you around, maybe my brother will lighten up some."

"I'm working on it," she responded.

"Now that the mutual admiration society is in session, can I kiss my sister goodbye?" I gave Lisa a long squeeze, then, as an afterthought, offered my hand to Mitch. "Mitch?"

We shook hands coolly as Mitch turned to Laurie. "We could use someone with your bounce in our next production. Think about it."

"Sorry, but I've already got a job for the summer," she smiled, leading me off toward the parking lot.

Once settled in the car, I put my arm around Laurie and drew her near. "I thought you got a curfew extension," I said.

"I did. But judging from the way you were acting, I'd thought you'd be uncomfortable going back to their cabin."

"You're too smart. What am I going to do with you?"

"What am *I* going to do with *you* is more like it." She pulled away from me. "You guys are something else. You think you can hit on any girl that comes along. Then your sister takes her life in her own hands and *you* want to send her off to a cloister. It's a double standard and I don't appreciate it." Then, folding her arms and glaring at me, she yelled, "You know what you are? You're a prude. You're actually a prude.... Your sister's great. She and I could get along real well."

We drove a few miles in silence then I began to laugh, slowly shaking my head side to side. "This is too funny. I bring you down here 'cause I want to show you off to my sister. The next thing I know, the two of you hit it off and I'm left out in the cold."

"Did you say you wanted to show me off? Am I a trophy or something?"

"You know what I mean. I'm proud of you. I like being with you...."

"But I don't belong to you."

After a long pause, I said, "That's true....... Gee, nothing that I say tonight seems to come out right."

"Try thinking before you talk. It helps." Laurie then looked at me, her eyes softening, "You know, I like you too. Very much. Maybe we're expecting too much. Let's go easy."

As the car entered Paradise Lake, I turned to Laurie, "There's a special place I want to show you."

"Now?" she asked, surprised.

"Sure. You still have that curfew extension, don't you?"

Looking at her watch, she said, "Another thirty minute's worth. You're the driver. I'm your captive."

I took the turn towards the Crystal Arms Hotel, then went off on a dirt road just before the wooden bridge. Looking around uncertainly, I said, "We might as well stop here. It's got to be close by."

"I thought you knew this place."

"Only by sea, my dear. Not by land. I found it by rowing across the lake. But it's got to be somewhere near here. Trust me." We took off our shoes and started walking, hand in hand. Soon we came over a bluff and the entire lake appeared, glistening in the half light of the moon.

"Oh, it's gorgeous, Phil," Laurie said, out of breath.

"Wait. Let's go over there by the oak tree." I ran ahead, then waited for her to scamper into my arms.

"Oh, it really is special," she said, nuzzling me back.

We stood together watching as the still water reflected both the soft clouds overhead and the yellow lights emitted from the fortress called the Crystal Arms Hotel.

# CHAPTER 22

It was times like this that made me want to whistle. But I had never learned how to do it right. I did, in fact, secretly envy anyone who could emit a full-throated quivering warble. But this was not to be for me. The best my body could do to reflect my present feeling of euphoria was to skip down the four flights of stairs to my morning venue of labor. Even the sight of Marty Gould could not temper my good mood. I went so far as to initiate a friendly greeting. "Hey, Marty, I saw you at the track the other night. I didn't know you were into the horses."

"Me? No, man. I don't go to the track," Gould said emphatically.

"What do you mean?" I asked incredulously. "I saw you. You were there with some guy in a green hat."

"No way. Couldn't have been me. I don't hang out with guys who wear green hats." Despite Gould's denial, I thought I detected a slight reddening in the rodent's face. Then Gould softened his stance. "You must've seen some other good looking guy," he smirked, and then walked away.

I pondered the brief conversation for a few minutes, shook my head, then ambled over to Stan's station. "You're not going to believe this," I began.

Without looking up, Stan said flatly, "You smashed up my car."

"No."

"You got a speeding ticket."

"No. I said unbelievable."

"You made out in the back seat and I need new upholstery."

"Get this." I paused to get Stan's attention. "Gould says he's never been to the track."

Stan stared at me. "Impossible. We saw him."

"I know. It's really weird. He even looked kind of funny when I mentioned the guy with the green hat."

"You know, now that you mention it, I've seen that hat somewhere else—but I don't know where," Stan mused.

"Anyhow, it's weird. What's he got to hide, anyway?"

"So nothing's wrong with my car? It's still in three pieces?"

"Your car was great. I even left you a few fumes in the gas tank."

"Now that's gratitude." Stan then lowered his voice and, knitting his eyebrows, said, "Listen, buddy. While you were out with Miss Wonderful, and me and Danny were in the casino last night, someone rifled through Danny's stuff. You should have heard him when we got back. He tried to put his fist through the wall—but I think he hit a stud. He'll be hurting this morning for sure."

"That guy's such a slob, how could he tell anyone was there?"

"He can tell," Stan responded.

"Anything gone?"

"Nothing that he knows about yet, but if it was money they were after, they were out of luck. He's real pissed off and as far as he's concerned, except for the two of us, no one's off the hook."

"Is he going to tell the Millers?" I wondered.

"Noooh!"

Danny walked into the dining room and marched directly over to Stan and me. "The fucker's dead," he declared.

"Who is it?" I asked.

"Whoever."

Stan rolled his eyeballs. "Are you going to shoot first and ask questions later? Don't be an asshole. Nothing's missing yet. Just stay cool and don't make too much noise. Let's keep our eyes open and, for now, let's all of us keep our doors locked. And don't tell anyone."

"Listen to the detective," Danny said, half surprised, half impressed. "I think the fucker was after money. Why me? Do I look like Daddy Warbucks?"

"Whoever it was, was probably just looking for an unlocked door," Stan said confidently. "Who's your room-mate?"

"Myron."

The three of us looked at each other. "Nah, he's too dumb," Stan declared.

"Maybe it was one of the dishwashers. They're always desperate for booze money," Danny speculated.

"Don't go off on a crazy witch-hunt now. You don't want to end up being sorry," I added.

"Yeah, yeah, you're right. But I tell you, the fucker's dead."

A voice boomed from across the dining room. "Are you gentlemen planning on working this morning or are our guests going to eat buffet style?" It was Mr. Arthur. We dispersed on cue, but he was not done. The maitre d' announced a meeting for mid-morning.

\* \* \*

It was a gray, overcast day, causing the breakfast guests to linger longer than usual. But by ten o'clock, the room was clear and Mr. Arthur clapped his hands, signaling everyone to gather 'round. "First order of business," he began, "-my bell. It shouldn't be necessary for me to clap my hands. The summer is well past the half way mark and my bell hasn't turned up yet. I am not happy about that." He looked around the group as if a conspiracy had been in the works.

Bobby Meyers whispered to me, "Should we take up a collection for the captain?"

"On a more positive note, I'm pleased to say that Mrs. Miller has no objections to the concept of an informational tipping sign. So, Dechter, you can proceed with the work." He started to turn towards the door, then hesitated. "One more thing," he said. "Koenig tells me his room was broken into last night and he's missing $40. I'm not a policeman. I'm just telling you so that you'll all be informed. Remember, tonight starts a big weekend. I want everyone clean, and clean-shaven. Especially you, Meyers—even if you have to shave three times before dinner. That's all I have." Then he left.

The staff eyed one another silently. Finally, Sid broke the ice. "There's something strange about his priorities, don't you think?"

"You might have something there," Sam added.

Feeling better about not being the only victim, Danny said, "Maybe whoever borrowed Murray's 40 bucks is out buying a new bell for the king."

"Yeah, sure," Stan said without a smile as the others laughed. He then followed Murray back to his station and confided, "You know, you're not the only one. Danny got hit last night too. But he didn't go off and tell the big man."

"You got a better idea? I'm the one who's out 40 bucks," Murray grumped.

"I'm workin' on it, cous. I'm workin' on it."

\* \* \*

That afternoon, I worked feverishly on the tipping sign so it would be ready for the large crowd coming in that night. All stations were expected to be filled to capacity. Shortly before dinner I hung my discreet artwork over the main desk, then stepped back to admire it. Joann Miller joined me. "Not bad for a pre-med," she said.

"Thanks. Now let's see if it does any good."

"By the way," she smiled, "there are big doings in the casino tomorrow night—including a dance contest. I'm not going to let this one get away. Can I count on you to be my partner?"

"Sorry, Joann. I'm afraid I've got other plans." Seeing her disappointment, I added, "But thanks for asking. I'm sure you'll knock 'em dead anyway." I gave her a soft punch in the shoulder, winked, then jogged off to the dining room, leaving her with hands on her hips and eyes glaring.

# CHAPTER 23

Other plans, indeed. I dressed hastily, then looked in the mirror and decided to wear a tie. I splashed a little *Canoe* on my cheeks, determined that this was going to be a romantic evening, without distractions. A late Saturday night dinner with Laurie. Yes, that would be special—and at one of those European restaurants in town that Sylvia recommended.

\* \* \*

The phone rang behind the front desk. "Crystal Arms Hotel—the heart of the Catskills," Joann answered automatically.

"May I speak to Phil Dechter, please? He's on the dining room staff," a feminine voice inquired.

"Who's calling, please?" Joann returned coolly.

"This is Laurie, a friend."

"I'm afraid Mr. Dechter isn't available. Can I leave a message?"

"Yes, it's very important. We're getting together tonight, but I won't be able to get out till half an hour after we're supposed to meet. Could you please let him know? I'd hate to have him waiting for nothing."

"Sure. He'll get the message," Joann said sweetly. After hanging up, she whispered to the phone, "Don't worry, dearie. He won't have to wait at all."

Diana Miller peered over her half glasses at her daughter and remarked with a sigh, "Are you about to do something bitchy that only a Miller woman would do?"

"I don't know what you're talking about," Joann said impatiently, then, eyeing Myron Smith across the lobby, summoned him over. "Be a sweetheart and run up to Phil's room," she began softly. "Tell him his date just called and had to cancel out for tonight."

"Sure," he said innocently, and trotted off to carry out his assignment.

"Don't look at me like that, Mom. You know I'm not a good student. Sometimes I get messages mixed up."

Myron Smith dashed up the stairway two steps at a time. As he made the turn at the second floor landing, he spotted Sylvia down the corridor carrying a large object. He quickly rerouted his steps and offered his assistance.

"Don't be silly, Myron," she scoffed. "It's only an extra speaker for the casino, and it's very light. I'm not a little flower, you know."

"Oh yes you are. I insist," he said, grabbing the speaker from her and almost knocking her over.

"You're too sweet," she managed, then led him down the hallway toward the other end of the building. Ten minutes later, as they passed an open window, Myron heard the rumbling of a defective muffler. Looking out, he saw a 1949 black Ford leaving the rear parking lot.

"Oh, shit," he gasped.

"What's wrong, Myron. Did you get a hernia?" Sylvia asked.

\* \* \*

I loved having access to the Simobile. Riding up the rocky road to Camp Tiroga, I promised myself to wash the car the next day to show Stan my appreciation. When I got to the gate, Laurie was not there. I started to pace, trying to conjure up reasons for her delay. Could she have stood me up? That wouldn't be like her. I was determined not to get angry. If only she would show up.

Laurie finally appeared, radiant in a simple red blouse and plaid skirt. I had never seen her in a skirt and the sight caused my eyes to light up. "You look great dressed up," I said.

"You clean up pretty well yourself," she countered. "You got my message, didn't you?"

"What message?"

"That I'd be late. Don't tell me you've been waiting here for half an hour."

"It's okay. I wanted to memorize all the license plates in the parking lot anyway."

"Poor baby," she said, holding my cheeks gently between her hands. "I guess we have saboteurs at both ends."

"We'll just have to try that much harder," I said. "...against the rain, the wind, the earthquakes.... and those bitches who answer the phones."

It was after 9 o'clock by the time Laurie and I arrived at the Lorelei. Hand in hand, we crossed over a short, dimly lit stone bridge separating the parking lot from the restaurant itself. Enticing smells greeted us as I opened the heavily carved wood entrance door. Looking around, we found the interior adorned with intricate chalet-like woodwork. While dark and rustic, the white tablecloths and amber glowing wall sconces gave the room an atmosphere of warmth and elegance. A small wiry man approached us with smiling silver teeth and showed us to a table overlooking a small pond. He bowed with European grace and left us with menus and the promise of a delightful evening. Sylvia had assured me that the cost would not be prohibitive, but seeing the well dressed and demure middle-aged clientele gave me reason to doubt it. Laurie caught a slight frown on my face and whispered, "This place looks expensive,.... but it's so charming."

I reached across the table and took her two hands in mine and smiled, "We're here. Let's enjoy it," and ordered two glasses of Dubonnet red.

"Everybody looks so continental," Laurie observed. "I'll bet we're the only ones here born in this country."

"Raising one eyebrow playfully, I said, "Speak for yourself, lady. I'm still a product of gay old Vienna." Seeing a shocked look on Laurie's face, I added, "Not by much. Just enough to be ineligible to run for President. Why else do you think I went into pre-med?" I laughed.

"You never told me," Laurie said, still shocked.

"Well, my family just managed to get out in time—right after Kristalnacht. I was only a few months old. That's the whole story."

"The whole story? You guys were refugees, forced to leave Europe—and there's no story? I don't believe it," she said wide-eyed.

"Well,.... sure, there were problems. My parents had to abandon everything, leave family. It's just that they never really got into it with me. They've always been vague about that time of their lives." I paused for a moment, then, "Actually, when I think about it, I've probably learned more about that time from some of the strangers I've met up here."

Laurie shook her head silently side to side. The drinks arrived. I raised my glass and cheerfully toasted, "Let's drink to the here and now." Laurie acquiesced.

From across the empty dance floor the shrill sound of a violin invaded the calm ambiance of the room. A short, hunched man appeared in tuxedo, flailing rhapsodically on his instrument, his deep, hollowed eyes closing with each thrust of his bow. He stopped at a nearby table and shifted his tempo to a waltz beat. After hovering over the diners for a few minutes, he snatched an outstretched dollar bill and moved on.

"Uh, oh," I whispered, "He's coming this way."

"How quaint," Laurie giggled.

The man bowed and addressed me in the most European of European accents, "Does the charming lady wish to hear a favorite tune?"

"Without hesitating, I responded, "Do you do any Sinatra?"

"I'm afraid not," he smiled unctuously and backed away.

"Oh, Phil," Laurie sighed when he was gone, "How crass!" Then, imitating the violinist, she added, "Why didn't you ask the charming lady what *she* wanted to hear?"

"And what would the charming lady have said?"

"Sinatra, of course," she laughed.

"Believe it or not, I was brought up on Beethoven. It's just that I hate these guys trying to embarrass me into spending money I didn't plan on. I know it looks cheap....... I'm sorry."

"Hey," she said, taking my hand. "Don't be sorry. I know you don't have much money to spend. In fact, I think our coming here in the first place is outrageous. I think you're precious for taking me. Let the older, suave continentals pay for the violin. They're the ones who love it. Look at them. Why is it that all the men look like Paul Henreid?"

"Suave, huh? Well, at least I still have all my hair."

"I didn't mean you weren't suave. To prove it, I'm going to let you order for me. With all that Viennese blood that's in your veins, I'm sure you'll know what's good."

"Fair enough." I waived to the waiter who, short of saluting, snapped to obsequious attention. I observed his starched white collar and silently lamented the sorry state of what passed for clean among my own dining room colleagues. I ordered sauerbraten with red cabbage for Laurie and, seeing Wiener schnitzel on the menu, could not help but be curious how it stacked up to my own mother's fine cooking. That done, I turned to Laurie and suggested we work up a little appetite for the treat to come by joining those "older sophisticates" slowly filling the dance floor.

We danced closely and quietly until Laurie whispered, "I feel like a voyeur in a foreign country watching people of a different station—even a different time. I see them as true romantics living in a world that's really lost forever."

"You're right. It seems like they froze Europe the way it was before the war—and won't let go. This is the way they had it and the way they want to keep it. So they brought it to the Catskills......I don't know if it's sad or admirable."

"But there was a war. Maybe they're blocking it out and just choosing to remember the good times.....Sort of like your parents."

"My parents? They'd just as soon forget everything, except for maybe the schnitzel. Let's go back to the table." I was getting hungry.

"I love this stuff," Laurie declared as she devoured the sauerbraten. "I've never had meat that melted in my mouth like this. You ordered just right. How's your dish?"

"The schnitzel's good. Not like my mother's, but good."

"Do you want to find life stories among our fellow diners?" Laurie asked with sly, wide-eyed glee.

"Here? We'd probably find more of my sister's secret boyfriends. Please, spare me."

Introduced by a simple piano roll, a petite blond woman wearing a light blue gown tip-toed to the center of the now empty dance floor and began to sing, "Wien, Wien, nor du allein......."

I leaned back in my chair and sighed, "It seems like a hundred years ago that I heard that song for the first time. Sylvia, our hotel hostess, does a better job, though. She puts more soul into it."

"I don't know German, but it sounds so nostalgic," Laurie whispered.

"Oh, it is. It is. It's all about Vienna, the city of remembered dreams and beautiful women."

When the applause for the song died down, Laurie announced, "This dinner is fabulous—and the evening's even better."

I smiled. "I'm glad you're having a good time. I really am. I've been looking forward to something like this." I then pursed my lips and nodded emphatically.

She laughed, "You're so serious."

"When they throw us in the kitchen, would you rather wash or dry?"

"Come on! *BE* serious. How's work at the sweat shop?"

"Actually, there's some weird stuff going on. A couple of the guys have had their rooms broken into and some money is missing."

"I hope you're not going to gang up on that one guy you and Stan don't like," she pleaded.

"We're not ganging up on anyone. It's just that things are tense right now and everyone's suspicious of everyone else. But speaking of our good friend Gould, he pulled a real strange one on me. He denies ever being at the track."

"That is strange," Laurie said, knitting her dark eyebrows.

"When I reminded him he was with an older man wearing a green Tyrolean hat, he got even more adamant."

"Wait a minute," Laurie interrupted.

"What?"

"That man was at the game."

"What game?"

"The softball game. I distinctly remember him sitting with your hotel owner's son. They were sitting apart from everyone else and he kept putting on and taking off that silly hat."

"What! That was the owner of the Matterhorn Hotel!" I said, almost shouting.

"Whoever it was, was the same guy at the race track." Laurie and I stared at each other.

"You don't realize what you've just told me." I closed my eyes and raised both hands as if to call time out. "Let me think this through. What you don't know is that Ron Miller and this Fritzie character had a pretty big money bet riding on this game. Now, when I think of Gould and the green yodeler at the track together, all kinds of possibilities come up."

"Like?"

"Like Gould was supposed to be a good ballplayer. But he goofed up so many plays, it's conceivable that he was trying to throw the game."

"You mean he might have been trying to pay off a gambling debt to his track buddy by making sure he'd win his bet?"

"Hey, you're way ahead of me," I said, wide-eyed. "This is great.... Now hold on. The only problem for Gould is—we win the game. Now he's really in the hole."

"Obviously, he doesn't want anyone to know that he knows Fritzie," Laurie added. "And he's desperate."

"So he's got to raise cash fast."

"So he tries to do it the old fashioned way—by stealing it."

"Right again, Nancy Drew." I grabbed Laurie's hands across the table and raised them, as in victory. "Wait a minute." I hesitated. "This all sounds good and comes to a dynamite conclusion, but it's only a theory. We can't prove any of it."

"True. You still have to catch him red-handed. But at least you now have a suspect."

"Yeah, well,.... I'll talk to Stan in the morning. Hey, I wanted this evening to be romantic. I didn't want to talk about problems at the hotel."

"Wait a minute," Laurie interrupted, her eyes lighting up. "This is fun. Didn't we solve a mystery—sort of?"

"Yeah."

"Well, to my way of thinking, that's very sexy."

Guided by a plump, rosy-cheeked woman wearing a white dirndl blouse and velvet jumper skirt, a dessert cart stopped at our table. Hypnotized, we simply stared at the contents. The woman smiled and broke the trance. "Does something appeal to you?" she twinkled in broken English.

"It all looks too good," Laurie responded, still mesmerized. "What are they?"

"We have a *Linzertorte,...Eclair...Apfelstrudel...Napolean...Sachertorte,...*"

"Stop right there," I interrupted. "We'll have the *Sachertorte—mit schlagobers.*"

"What's that?" gasped Laurie.

"*Schlagobers,*" I repeated, pausing with great satisfaction, "is whipped cream—but when you say '*Schlagobers*', it tastes much, much better."

Laurie was presented with a dense, triangular solid of chocolate covered chocolate cake, bisected by a single layer of raspberry jam. The waitress then cast a huge dollop of rich whipped cream at its center, transforming the innocent looking geometric shape into something Laurie could only describe as "sinful."

# CHAPTER 24

Perhaps it was the rich chocolate that wouldn't let me sleep. Or maybe the anxiety of our findings about Gould. At any rate, I climbed out of bed early the next morning with my head still throbbing. I staggered down the corridor to Stan's room and knocked. Without saying a word and looking no better in his jockey shorts than I felt, a groggy Stan waved me in. Also still in my skivvies, I carefully closed the door and sat down at the end of Stan's cot. "Can anyone hear us?" I whispered.

"What's the matter, lover-boy?" Stan growled, his eyes glazed over. "You turning queer on me? Couldn't you get anything last night?"

"Just shut up and listen," I insisted, still in a hushed voice.

"Okay, what's up?" he asked, scratching his unruly head of hair and becoming slightly more alert. Motionless, Stan listened as I related my conversation with Laurie and Gould's connection to Fritzie Baumgarten. Then, "Holy shit! Why didn't we think of that?"

"The question is, 'What are we going to do about it?'"

"Let me wash my face. It makes me think fast." Stan stuck his head in his tiny sink and let cold water run over it. He stooped there for over five minutes until I thought he might have fallen asleep and drowned. Then he emerged, shaking his dripping locks and beaming a strange smile. "Got a plan."

"What?"

"First off, I gotta tell ya—whatever happens, I hope Ron never finds out about Fritzie. The dogfight between these two hotels would make the Civil War look like a panty raid."

"Okay, okay."

Stan sat back on his cot, put a towel over his head and spoke through it. "We set the guy up. If he passes, nothing lost. If he bites, we nail him."

"What are you talking about?"

"Whose station does he go by on the way to the kitchen?"

"Sid's and then Murray's," I answered dutifully.

"Forget Murray. He's been had. Sid's perfect," Stan said, ripping the towel away. "Gould thinks Sid's a real lunch bag, right? That's good. We've got to get hold of Sid and get his cooperation—but without his busboy's help. Danny might just screw things up with his hot head. We've got to pull this off after lunch, right after the great exodus. In the meantime, collect as many one-dollar bills as you can."

"You haven't told me the plan."

"That's okay. I'll explain it to you and Sid at the same time," a wide-awake Stan declared, looking me straight in the eye. "Let's go!"


When I got to the dining room Myron Smith was waiting at my station. "I'm real sorry about last night," he said sheepishly.

"What are you talking about?" I asked in annoyed confusion. Ever since I woke up, everyone seemed to be talking to me in riddles.

"I didn't get the message to you about your date in time. I'm sorry you had to drive all the way there for nothing."

"Don't take it so hard, Myron. It wasn't for nothing. I just had to wait a little bit, that's all."

"But Joann said she cancelled out."

"That's interesting......Thanks for the information," I said, angry but bemused. Myron walked away, shaking his head in bewilderment.

On the look-out for Sid, I caught Joann's eye instead. She looked away and headed toward Mr. Arthur. "Hey, Joann," I yelled, feeling my face turn hot. "How'd you do in the dance contest?"

"I didn't win, if that's what you're asking," she said defensively.

"Good!" I shouted, and turned away, not wanting to see her reaction.

"My, my," Sam said quietly from the corner of the station. "Aren't we playing a little bit with fire?"

"I don't give a shit. She tried to sabotage me." I was surprised at my own rage.

"Ah, the love triangle," Sam sighed to the goblets. "It will outlast all the wars—and do just as much damage."

I didn't have time for this. I knew something was going to happen this day, but didn't think it would involve my love life. One thing was for sure—with a full weekend like this, the staff expected a big pay-off after lunch. Everyone moved a little quicker and looked a little sharper. Even Bobby Meyers, in his quest to be clean shaven, sported three little tufts of tissue paper on his face to absorb the blood of his efforts. And, of course, the tipping sign had not yet been tested. Anxiety hung in the air.

Looking around, I found all the players in the room. Stan and Sid were off in one corner and Gould was going about his business as usual. I joined the twosome. "I don't like it. It's too chancy," I heard Sid say.

"Don't worry. Look, here's Phil. You respect him. It was his idea. He wouldn't do anything crazy. Would you, Phil?" Stan asked rhetorically. "Besides, you hardly have to do anything. Between the three of us we've got to accumulate a wad of singles—say at least thirty. Get what you can to me before lunch. Leave the rest to me." Not a sound from his partners. "By the way, keep strict accounts. You'll get it back...... Thanks for the input, Phil. Gotta run.... Have a good meal, guys." The two of us watched as Stan jogged off to his station.

Sid turned skeptically to me and asked, "Was this really your idea?"

"Yeah," I lied. Then I, too, walked away.

The breakfast menu alone reflected the import of the day. Aside from the usual assortment of appetizers which included both creamed and matjes herring, fried herring had been added as a special attraction. Mr. Arthur alerted the busboys that there might be a run on this delicacy, and warned us not to horde the treat at our stations. But by the time the first guests arrived, very little fried herring could be found in the kitchen, as many a monkey dish of the stuff found its way to closed silverware drawers in various stations throughout the room.

Sam always made it his business to find out which guests from our station might be leaving after breakfast. Not only would he give them extra attention, but also keep an eye on them, lest they forget to pay due homage. With my obligation to fulfill my quota of one-dollar bills, I was particularly keen on sharing in the vigil. As luck would have it, I did better than I had hoped, but most of my tips were in increments of five dollar bills. Not wanting to involve other waiters and busboys, I was forced to retreat to the lobby in search of change. Joann was behind the desk, checking out departing guests. I waited for a break, then quickly approached. "I need some singles for three fives," I snapped.

"Why should I do you any favors?" she countered. "You really embarrassed me in the dining room."

"Don't give me that crap, Joann. You know what you did."

"How many singles did you say?" she asked, avoiding my eyes.

"Fifteen."

"I didn't know you were a poker player."

"I'm not. But your guests are so damn cheap, they expect change when they tip." I didn't relish maligning my patrons but it was the only way I could think of getting the needed results and hurting her at the same time.

"I'm really sorry if the sign doesn't work," she said in a soft, sincere tone. Now it was me who felt too guilty to meet her eyes. I made the exchange, said thanks, and darted back to the dining room.

All guests were gone. Stan and Bobby Meyers were seated at their station—one counting money, the other licking his fingers. "This fried herring is good stuff," Bobby said, seeing me approach. "Did you have any?"

"No, the guests wanted it all."

"Schmuck! Here, have one, I've had four already. If Arthur passes by, he'll smell me out for sure."

"Thanks. Anything to help out." I took the dish and looked at Stan. "How'd you make out?"

"So far, so good, buddy. Come, let's take a walk," he said, leading me over to Sid's station.

Sid met us halfway, quickly pressing a roll of bills into Stan's hand. "That's eight. I only had one couple leave. I'm sorry," he said.

"I've got seventeen," I added.

"Great. We're over the top," Stan whispered, scrunching our contributions into his pocket. "Sometime at the end of lunch I'm going to plant the money on top of your station, Sid. Keep Danny busy and away from there." He looked us both in the eye, shrugged, then walked away, saying, "We'll see what happens."

If any guests had left in the morning, they were replaced by noon. Not a spare setting could be found in the dining room. As Sam pointed out to me, as he often did, "This meal is going to be another doozy." Not that steak would be a hard choice. Only those without sturdy teeth would pick the flanken. It was that steak had to be broiled on the spot, and with a full house, there would be long steamy lines in the kitchen and many hungry people in the dining room. And god forbid, someone requesting well-done should get a rare piece of meat. Then, to top it off, the Sunday dinner always included two desserts—first watermelon, to freshen the palette, then strudel, to stuff it. All designed for a warm send-off and, hopefully as a bi-product—good tips. Of the forty people at my station, twenty-eight were scheduled to leave after the noon meal, and all but eight of those had been at the hotel at least a full week. Between promising early reactions to our tipping sign and a lot of praying, I hoped to clear over one hundred dollars before the day was done.

As hectic as the 'doozy' played itself out, I tried to keep an eye out for Gould. Each time I passed through the swinging door from the kitchen to the dining room, I focused on Gould's station. Sometimes he was there, sometimes he wasn't. I also glanced towards Sid's area. All seemed normal—until strudel time. Sam was happily distributing the morsels to our flock when it seemed that all forty patrons demanded coffee at once. I lost complete track of my vigil. I poured and poured and poured. Then, racing into the kitchen for what I hoped would be the last refill of my silver coffee pot, I was stopped by Sid. "It's gone," the pre-lawyer whispered, staring wide-eyed through his misty spectacles.

"You sure?"

"Very sure."

"I'll tell Stan," I said coolly, and continued to the coffee machine. As the urn emptied its goods into my silver pot, my heart started to pound furiously. It was as if huge doses of caffeine were being deposited directly into my own veins. Something was going to happen. Yet when I told Stan the money was taken, all Stan said was "Good," rather matter-of-factly. I then returned to my station and attended to my main function. The drama would be out of my hands and in Stan's alone. Once again I would be a spectator to whatever was to unfold.

Lingering over their coffee, my guests were being particularly chatty, many engaging me in school-related conversation. I took this as a positive sign and embraced each opportunity to put in my two cents, hoping to get four. Word had gotten out that I had been responsible for the tipping sign. Anyone who commended me for it, I figured, would be good for at least the minimum suggested. On the other hand, someone offended by the sign would also act accordingly. So I hoped and chatted and smiled. And just as suddenly as their collective appetite for coffee made itself known, so did my guests' need to leave the dining room all at one time.

The tips came in a virtual shower—in crisp fives, in scrunched ones, and in secretive envelopes. It reminded me of my Bar Mitzvah. Then it was over. And as rapidly as my station emptied, so did the rest of the dining room. Mr. Arthur left with the last group of diners, closing the French doors from the lobby side.

Quickly, each member of the dining staff found a private spot at his station and started to count his take. Between my tips from the morning and what I could retrieve from my lint infested pockets, I had amassed one hundred and seven dollars. "All right!" I yelled, then held my breath as I saw Stan approach Gould's station.

"Hey, Marty," Stan called out louder than necessary. "You got change for a twenty? I need a bunch of singles for a card game."

"Yeah, maybe," Gould mumbled.

"Great." Stan watched as the rodent extracted a fat wallet from his back pocket. "Looks like you made out okay for the weekend," he added.

"Fair." Their eyes met suspiciously. Sid and I inched closer to the proceedings as Gould began to dole out his cache of ones. Stan took his allotment and immediately inspected each bill with great care.

"What the fuck are you doing?" Gould railed. "I don't print the stuff."

"I know you don't," Stan said softly, looking him squarely in the eye. Then, pointing to a little red "s" in the lower right hand corner of two consecutive bills, he shouted, "BUT I DO!" He then unleashed a powerful fist to Gould's jaw, sending him crashing into two chairs. Stan pounced on him again, yelling, "You motherfucking thief!"

Gould tried to defend himself, but was no match for an obsessed Stan Simon. Seeing the others gathered around by now, he pleaded with them, "Get him off me. He's nuts!" No one moved.

Stan continued his barrage. "This is for Murray.... This is for softball...."

"What the hell are you talking about?" Gould whined through the blood running from his nose.

Stan picked him up by the shirt collar and delivered one more blow to the midsection. "And that's for Tom Jamieson the third." Gould wilted to the floor. Stan stood up, rubbing his fist and breathing heavily. He warned, "You better get your ass out of here....... before we kill you....... There's no room around here for a fucking thief."

Panting, Gould got to his knees attempting to retrieve the bills scattered about. Stan made sure to retain all the marked ones, leaving his victim to grovel for the rest. I picked up Gould's wallet from the floor. It was almost empty except for the recognizable oval outline of a well-preserved "Trojan," the badge of any self-respecting New York warrior. I tossed the limp leather gently in Gould's direction.

No one spoke as Mr. Arthur re-entered the room. "I heard a little commotion. Is everything under control?" he asked, ignoring the upturned furniture.

Gould got up. "I quit!" he declared, wiping his face and still heaving. "I can't work with these animals." He handed the maitre d' a bloodied linen napkin and hobbled out.

Mr. Arthur dropped the napkin daintily to the floor and studied the staff. "It looks like we'll be short for dinner tonight," he said calmly. "Koenig, do you think you can pick up what's left of Mr. Gould's station?"

"Sure thing, sir."

"Good. Make sure things are straightened up before you all leave." Without further questions, he, too, left the room.

"Goddamn," Stan sighed with a shake of his head. "That dandy-ass has a sense of justice after all. He knows damn well there's at least forty bucks sitting at Gould's station in accounts receivable. See, Murray? You'll get it all back—plus some."

"What about me?" complained Danny. "You didn't even give him a whack for messing up my room."

"What are you talking about," Stan smiled. "He did you a favor. Your place never looked so good."

With the tension somewhat relieved, everyone chipped in to help restore the dining room to its former floor plan. "You did well, Stan," Sid commended.

"It's a good thing our hunch was right. Otherwise I'd have looked like a damn fool."

"I'm glad he's gone. That asshole gave me the creeps," offered Bobby Meyers. "What d'ya say we all go out tonight for a drink and celebrate. We all made out pretty good today, didn't we?"

"Yeah!" Danny supported the idea with great enthusiasm. "Now that we don't have any more thieves around here—except for you, Myron. I saw you take my last strudel." He then grabbed Myron Smith in a headlock and playfully rubbed a knuckle in his scalp.

Within half an hour, the dining room was cleared and set for dinner. In good spirits, most everyone was anxious to leave and take a well deserved afternoon break. Seeing Sam sit down with a freshly lit cigarette, I lingered behind and joined him. "You got a minute?" I asked.

"For you, Boychik, I've got three minutes. I see a frown on your handsome punim. What's on your mind?"

I sat down and started to fidget with a napkin. "Everyone's so glad this business is over and that Gould is gone. I'm relieved too, but somehow I feel very sad. Does that make any sense?"

"To me it does. I feel sad too."

"Really? Do you know why?"

"Yes." Sam exhaled a long stream of smoke and looked at me. "Here we have a young Jewish boy, not so different than yourself. But something is very wrong. He doesn't trust anybody and everyone else hates him. He needs money—like everybody else—but there's something desperate with him. He has lost contact with people, and so he turns against them. What's sad is that we don't know the end of the story. He leaves us as an unredeemed soul."

"Yeah," I said slowly, nodding my head in agreement, amazed that this old man can see things so clearly.

"Marty reminds me of someone from a long time ago." Sam said, looking off in a distant gaze. "Someone very unpleasant—also Jewish. I don't know how much you know about the concentration camps. It wasn't just Nazi soldiers in charge. They selected certain Jews to keep the rest of us in check. They were called Kapos. A few were kind but many of them thought the more brutal they treated us, the safer their own skin would be. In those days you did unthinkable things to survive. But to play the devil? Just to survive in hell? I don't know. To me, it's not worth it. There was this one fellow. His name was Mendel. He was a nasty one. I could tell when it was going to be a bad day. He would not look anyone in the face—just beat them like they didn't exist as people. I would try to catch his eye—stare into his soul to remind him he was a Jew. He knew what I was doing and didn't like it one bit. One day he told me that if I looked at him again, he would kill me. Ha! I didn't push my luck. I wanted to survive too." Sam shook his head. "Mendel, the Kapo. If he survived the war, I don't know if he could survive himself....... Unredeemed......... Better to die a mensch."

We two sat quietly, pondering the story. Then Sam startled me. "Look who's talking? What have I done?" he shrugged. "I survived,.... Big deal."

"You're a good man, Sam."

"We need people like Stanley, men of action...... He should go to Israel."

"I thought you didn't like Stan," I said.

"He may be a little bit crude, but he has honor and is a man of action—a good man."

"I agree," I nodded.

"But don't tell him I said so," Sam warned, raising his forefinger.

# CHAPTER 25

Poppy's was hopping. College kids from the local hotels streamed in in droves, looking to let off steam pent up over one of the busiest weekends of Paradise Lake's summer. I was there too, but not up to the exuberance of my cohorts. While they were lifting beer after beer in honor of Stan's heroics, I kept my eye peeled on the door, waiting for Laurie and her crew to arrive. When they did appear, Laurie, too, scanned the crowd, hesitant to enter the room without seeing me. Our eyes connected, and automatically we walked toward each other. Meeting on the dance floor in the middle of Johnny Mathis' "Chances Are," we melted into another's arms, dancing slowly and not saying a word. When the song was done, I suggested we go outside, saying the air and all the people around us were stifling.

Once on the sidewalk, I drew in a deep breath and put both hands on Laurie's waist. Looking into her eyes, I said, "I only want to be with you. Can we get away from our friends? Maybe take a walk or something?"

"That would be nice," she said softly.

"Tell your protectors that I'll get you back to camp somehow."

Within a few minutes we were walking hand in hand down the main road, the crowds thinning as we distanced ourselves from Poppy's. "You know," I began, "the first time I walked down this street, I thought it was the loneliest place I've ever seen. Right now, if you took all the other people away, it would be just right."

"You mean just you and me?" she asked, raising her dark eyebrows.

"Exactly. The perfect population."

"Isn't that a bit exclusive?"

"Yup. I just want to be with you," I said, squeezing her hand.

"You're acting strange tonight."

"It's been a strange day. Marty Gould is no longer with us, as they say in the business world."

"What happened? Oh, my god. Is it my fault?" Laurie clutched her throat.

"Fault? Thanks to you, it's all over. Stan set him up by marking some bills and then leaving them on an open station. Gould took the bait and Stan nailed him. Boy, did Stan nail him."

"Really? Wow! Leave it to Mr. Tough Guy to get the job done."

"You don't think I could have done it?" I asked, defensively.

"Probably not," Laurie said without hesitation. "You're a different kind of person. You can't do everything. But I like you just the way you are. You won't find me running off with a Stan Simon."

"Are we running off?" My face expressed exaggerated glee.

"Not exactly, but we are walking pretty far from where we started."

We found ourselves at the end of town facing the bridge toward the Crystal Arms. "Let's keep going," I urged. "It's such a gorgeous night. There's something special in the air—besides your perfume. And the moon. I'll bet it looks beautiful from the spot we visited that night.... Let's go."

Laurie and I continued over the bridge and went off the dirt road— and again took off our shoes. The cool wild grass felt both sensuous and comforting as we worked our way up the knoll. When we arrived at the great oak, gauzy clouds passed over the moon to greet us.

"Magnificent," Laurie managed, barely breaking the spell.

"You're magnificent," I whispered, standing behind her and kissing the top of her head. She turned around and leaned into me with her full body. We kissed. I pulled her gently down to the ground and kissed her again. We lay on the grass, locked together, and stared at the heavens.

"The first time I was here," I began wistfully, "I tried to imagine someone like you with me. Now it's like a dream come true." I rolled to my side and enveloped her in my arms, first kissing her lips, then her neck. My heart started to pound wildly as every nerve ending in my body came to life. Laurie put her hands between us as if in protest, but I could feel her heart pounding as well.

"Easy," she whispered. But my body was in a different mode. Groping under her sweater, I found both delight and encouragement to pursue further pleasure. To my surprise, her fervor equaled mine. When she finally murmured, "We have to stop," there was no stopping. Our bodies melded.

"I love you," I breathed as our passion became fulfilled. Then we lay there. Sweating and heaving, we smiled at each other, then collapsed in each other's arms again.

"You didn't use anything, did you?" Laurie asked, knitting her full eyebrows together.

"I'm sorry," I panted. "I didn't have time. It'll be all right."

"I hope so." We kissed again, then sat up. The moon was still there, but many clouds had passed.

"I can't believe we made love," I said stupidly, staring at the lake below.

"Believe it," Laurie answered nervously. "It's my fault. I let us go too far."

"Fault? There's no fault. I've dreamed about this for weeks. You're fabulous."

"I've got to go." Laurie got up abruptly and adjusted her jeans and sweater. She tried to laugh, "I'll never get the grass out of my hair."

"Let me help," I offered.

"No! I'll do it." She ran a comb through her hair with brisk strokes, staring at the flattened grass where we had made our indelible impression.

"You're not mad at me, are you?"

"I'm not mad at you," she repeated.

"Are you sorry?"

"I hope not."

We walked back across the meadow in silence. Just before reaching the road, I looked back. For just a moment, the fortress across the lake looked more like a prison than a hotel.

Retracing our steps through town, we decided not to go back to Poppy's, choosing instead to walk the full distance back to camp. We ambled through the quiet streets, hand in hand, until Laurie said, "I take back what I said."

"What?"

"I *am* sorry."

"Sorry? You shouldn't be."

"You sound just like..."

"What?"

"Forget it...... Everything's different now."

"It's better now," I insisted.

"No it's not."

"I meant what *I* said back there."

"What?"

"I love you."

"You just think you love me," Laurie said, intent on kicking a pebble straight up the road.

# CHAPTER 26

The middle of August meant one thing at Camp Tiroga—and with that one thing came tension, exhilaration, tears and sleepless nights. Color War! Divided into two factions, the Blue and the Gold, both campers and counselors would compete on all fronts, from sports to songwriting, for four intense days and nights. Well in advance of the actual event, rumors would run rampant as to when and how Color War would "break."

One sweltering Tuesday, as the camp was struggling through an uninspired midday meal of macaroni, cheese, white bread and red bug juice, a commotion began in the middle of the dining hall. It seemed that someone had dropped a pitcher of the red stuff and it splattered almost an entire bunk of twelve year olds. Their counselor, Jack Rappaport, took exception with the counselor at the next table and a loud argument ensued. Jack stood on his chair so he could be eye to eye with big Jerry, the overgrown farm boy from the Bronx. As the two went at each other, the whole room drew to a bewildered hush. More than being surprised that the diminutive Jack should take on someone of Jerry's girth, the surrounding kids were shocked that the behemoth would talk back to the owner's son at all.

"You clumsy oaf!" railed Jack.

"Who you calling names, you little runt?" Jerry retaliated.

"This means war!" Jack shouted.

"What kind of war?" Jerry roared back on cue.

"There's only one kind," Jack declared, looking intently around the hall. "COLOR WAR!" He then jumped into Jerry's outstretched arms. Yelling together, they repeated, "THIS IS COLOR WAR!"

Mayhem broke loose as the 1957 campaign officially began. In a far corner of the room Laurie Stillman turned to her co-counselor, "Leave it to Jack to play hero."

"Yeah," Barb agreed, "at Jer's expense, too."

"I guess it comes with the territory. I wonder if all camp-owners' kids are born jerks."

That afternoon, lists of the warring factions were posted. Kids either squealed with delight in finding themselves paired with their buddies, or sobbed in despair as many friendships were put in temporary suspension. The leadership of each team was put in the hands of two Generals, male and female counselors pre-elected by the Counsel of Judges for their ability to fire up their troops and inspire performance. Laurie was chosen to lead the women of Gold. Her counterpart was General Jack Rappaport.

Among the side effects of Color War, to the benefit of some, and detriment to others, was loss of communication with the outside world. Notices extolling the virtues of Color War were sent to parents, assuring them that the isolation required for its success was a character-builder for the kids and not to worry. But for the counselors it created other problems. Except for dire emergencies, there was to be no contact made outside of camp for the duration, beginning at sundown that day.

\* \* \*

Just before dinner Laurie raced to the office phone to warn me, hoping she would not hear Joann Miller's voice at the other end. "Crystal Arms

Hotel, heart of the Catskills," Joann greeted her. When told I was already working in the dining room, Laurie left the message, ending with a plea "not to screw this up." Joann was more than happy to convey her message accurately. But I didn't believe her and tried to call the camp. When Laurie's inaccessibility was confirmed, I grudgingly apologized, citing Joann's recent track record.

I figured four days shouldn't be that bad, but, after just one day, I was surprised at how much I missed Laurie. After brooding away my first free evening thinking about our blissful moment on the bluff across the lake, I decided to revisit the site. The next afternoon I took out a rowboat and retraced my path, trying to recapture the feeling of that first day of discovery. But it was mid-August now and the day was cooler and the sky was overcast and somehow, I felt a little older. Heading into a stiff breeze though, I found the rowing invigorating, reminding me of the euphoria that particular exercise brought. Panting slightly, I climbed the hill and found the oak tree—as majestic a sight as ever. My first impulse was to carve a remembrance into its bark, but better judgment told me that was too trite for such a sacred living thing. Better to leave it unscathed, without my imprint. Looking around to make sure no one was watching, I put my arms around its huge trunk and closed my eyes, embracing my self-appointed symbol of everything pure and good. Then I sat on the grass and tried to remember the exact sequence of my love-making with Laurie. I could not. I sniffed the air but her perfume escaped me.

\* \* \*

Color War was all about spirit, teamwork, determination—and above all, talent. The Gold team had much of the ingredients but its dual leadership was a match made in the front office, rather than in heaven. While Laurie tried to organize her troops and inspire a winning attitude, Jack abdicated his role to his lieutenants, choosing rather, at this late time in the season, to make his move on his co-leader. Taking advantage of the time expected for them to be together planning their strategies, he forced his attentions on her, making her job almost impossible to carry out. Totally disinterested, and finally brought to tears, Laurie threatened to quit camp, Color War and all, unless he behaved himself. Rather than have his parents find out about his "bad luck," he acquiesced, promising to be a good boy and pull his own weight. But the campers as well as the other counselors had little respect for him and his efforts were in vain. The entire burden of carrying the Gold team fell on Laurie's shoulders. By the third day she was exhausted and had lost her voice to laryngitis.

\* \* \*

It was one of those steamy late summer afternoons. I chose to walk down to the lake where I saw a goodly number of the hotel clientele lining the shore. They were either sitting on benches or on neat blankets, watching the few active vacationers actually swimming in the water. I noticed the solitary figure of a young girl playing under the shade of a distant group of pine trees. Silently, I went over and observed her carefully arranging pine cones in several rows. She then proceeded to skip over them.

Shana Shechtman glanced up and smiled. "Good Shabbos, Mr. Phil."

"Same to you, Shana," I reacted, not immediately connecting this sultry Friday afternoon with the upcoming Sabbath. "How come you're playing here by yourself? Aren't there other kids down by the lake?"

"It's nice here," she answered shyly. "Besides, I don't know them."

I found it curious, on a hot summer day in the middle of a mountain resort area, that this child should be dressed in a long sleeved blouse and long skirt. "Do you like the water?" I asked carefully.

"Yes. I even know how to swim."

"That's great! Would you like to go in with me?"

She hesitated nervously. "I don't think so," then added, "but thank you."

Seeing this strange but bright young girl uncomfortable with my questions, I was about to leave, then decided to try one more. "Will you teach me your game?"

"Sure," she said, matter-of-factly, and promptly picked up a stick and drew a line in the pine-needle ground cover. She then handed me a pine cone and instructed me to stand behind the line. "Listen carefully," she ordered in a motherly tone, raising her forefinger for emphasis. "Throw the ball in the first row—if you can. Then, jump in that row, pick up the ball and jump in the next row. But you can't touch the walls. If you do, you're out."

"Walls?" I asked innocently.

"These, silly," she responded impatiently, pointing to the pine cones defining the rows.

"Okay, I've got it. Can I try now?"

"Yes, you can *try*," she said, accenting the last word.

I did as instructed and as I stood poised in the second row waiting for further directions, I heard clapping coming from behind a cluster of high shrubs. Out emerged a laughing Sam Shechtman. His stunted form stood in the opening with his arms folded triumphantly over his white shirt and his face beaming. "You take better instructions from my daughter than you do from me," he chuckled.

"We were just having a little fun," I said, both embarrassed and pleased that Sam had spied on our little encounter.

"Poppa," Shana interrupted, "you're spoiling our game."

"Sorry, Tatteleh. I'm trying to save Phil from certain defeat." Shana skewered her face as he continued, "Shaneleh, Mama needs you right now to help with the Shabbos candles. Go back to the house. I'll be there in a jiffy."

After thanking me for playing with her, Shana kissed her father and was off. "She's a real doll," I said, as we watched her skip away through the trees.

"As I told you, she's my life," Sam sighed.

Waiter and busboy stood together at the edge of the woods, our black and white uniforms in sharp contrast to the deep earthy hues behind us. I picked up a pine cone and tossed it at a prominent blue spruce thirty yards away. When it hit its target, I declared, "That's for Mr. Feigenbaum, for stiffing me last week."

Sam laughed, "There aren't enough trees in the forest for all the times I've been stiffed."

"Aw, come on," I smiled. "Everybody loves you. Why would anybody stiff you?"

"Like everything else, you do what you have to do. If you're short on cash, you don't pay what's not required. There's no law that says you have to tip. They can love you, but love is cheap. Remember that, boychik." I nodded with a frown. "Speaking of love," Sam continued, "how's your pretty girlfriend?"

"She's fine but I haven't seen her in four days. They've got this stupid thing called Color War at her camp and she's totally isolated till it's over. I'll be glad when the summer's done and there won't be any more dumb barriers."

"Be patient. In ten days it will all be over. You will have made your fortune. You won't have me to badger you any more. And you'll have your honey to chase all over New York."

"It sounds good but I know I'll miss you. Despite my complaining it really has been a great summer."

"Now that's what I like to hear," Sam said warmly, patting me on the shoulder.

"Sam, can I ask you something personal?"

"Personal? Nothing is more personal than a waiter and busboy working together. Go ahead, ask!" he said, promptly lighting up a cigarette.

"It's about Shana." Sam exhaled slowly and widened his eyes. I continued, "She's really a great kid."

"You said that already. That's not a question."

"I was just wondering. Does she have many friends?"

"She has plenty of friends at school," Sam scoffed, squinting in his own smoke.

"But it's summertime. I see kids playing down by the lake, but I never see her with them. Is she shy?"

"Shana is different. We are different," Sam said deliberately. "Our daughter goes to a religious school just for girls. She learns about the world as I knew it—the way I would like to see it. I think other people call it 'traditional'. We lost a lot with Hitler, but we didn't lose everything. So some of us must preserve a certain way of life. It's not for everyone. But it must be for me." I nodded slowly as Sam continued. "If I, who was chosen to survive, should forget my past, then all is lost. So, my friend, you will forgive me if Shana is a little different from the other children. A long answer to a short question, no?"

"Thanks," I said sheepishly. "She's still a great kid."

"Come," Sam said, patting me again on the shoulder. "I have to make Shabbos with my family before we feed the masses. I'll see you in the salt mines." He waived with his cigarette and soon disappeared down the wooded path.

Alone again, I watched the scene down by the lakefront. It reminded me of a Seurat painting studied in my first year Fine Arts class. It was entitled "Sunday Afternoon On The Island Of The Grande Jatte." There was a quiet formality common to both the people in the work of art and the ones I was observing in reality before me. It occurred to me that Europeans don't know how to be casual—that it must take two generations on American soil before someone learns how to loosen up.

# CHAPTER 27

"It was a disaster," her hoarse voice croaked as we sat by the camp gate, the cool evening breeze hinting at the closing days of August.

"I really missed you," I said, putting my hands gently on Laurie's shoulders.

"Did you hear what I said? We lost!"

"You really care that much about stupid Color War?"

"Yes, I care!" she huffed, standing up and circling me with her arms folded. "People depended on me and we blew it. Now they'll spend the whole winter moping about losing."

"Aren't you exaggerating?" I scoffed. "I'm sure they'll all find something else to worry about the minute they get home from camp. Besides, it wasn't your fault. You tried your best and I'm sure they all still love you—just like I do—even though you sound like a frog." I got up and wrapped my arms around her waist.

"You're sweet," she purred. "But do you have any sense of the responsibility it takes to lead a hundred kids whose hearts are set on winning?"

"Hey, I don't want to argue with you. This is probably our last night together up here. I'd like it to be special."

"Me too. But not *too* special," Laurie warned with a sly sideward glance.

We walked down the road, then slowly along the creek where we spent our first evening together so many cool, pine-scented nights before. I put my sweater over her shoulders, then guided Laurie across the stepping stones. When we reached the bridge I took both her hands and looked into her eyes. "I'm really looking forward to being together in the city. I know you're going to give me a hard time about this but I've got to be honest. I really want to show you off to my fraternity brothers."

"What if my voice doesn't come back?"

"Even if you sound like a frog forever." I kissed her gently, then again with more passion.

"You know," she interrupted, "it's going to be different in the city."

"Why should that be?"

"It always is—that's all," she shrugged.

"If anything, there'll be more stuff to do. It'll be great. I can't wait. I wish Labor Day were tomorrow so we could get a head start."

"Hey, busboy, you'd better wait out the whole season and make all the money you can if you want to afford taking me out." Laurie chuckled and planted her full lips on mine.

* * *

Three days later the busses rolled out of Camp Tiroga, ending the 1957 summer season. While I went through the motions of my daily chores, my heart was elsewhere, chugging along the thruway with a bunch of kids and their beautiful, fallen general. Yet I was determined to finish my job honorably—and with cash in my pockets.

The Friday before Labor Day, Diana Miller summoned me into her office. Closing the door, she wasted no time. "You know you've made this summer miserable for my daughter," she said, looking coldly into my eyes.

"I don't know about that," I responded weakly, trying to avoid her glare.

"Don't get coy with me, young man." She then proceeded to unbutton her blouse. I watched in amazement as she removed it and then unhooked her bra. With a quizzical smile she stood bare-breasted, waiting for my reaction.

"What are you doing?" I managed, re-faced.

"Oh, I've already done it," she stated with defiance. "What are you going to do?"

With my heart pounding, I studied the pattern in the throw rug beneath me. "Nothing," I whispered finally.

She shook her head in disgust, her ample breasts swaying in agreement. "You're such a little boy. I don't know what Joann sees in you."

I looked around, desperately in search of relief. "What are you trying to do, humiliate me?" I mumbled.

Smiling, she repeated, "Humiliate you? Why—do you feel humiliated?"

"Yes."

"Good! Now get out of here," she ordered, "and finish off the week. Don't bother to tell anyone about this. No one will believe it."

"*I* don't believe it," I muttered, and grasped for the doorknob.

\* \* \*

The welcome sight of Sam and his goblets greeted me as I entered the dining room. "What's the matter, boychik? You look like you've seen a ghost."

"At least one," I replied, walking past him and into the kitchen. Ignoring Wanda, I went directly to the scuzzy little bathroom in the corner and closed the door. Looking in the mirror, I saw a shaken little boy. "What the fuck did she expect me to do?" I said aloud, slamming my fist on the stained porcelain sink. I then let cold water run over my hands and pressed them to my face. "Just three more days," I thought.

Sam was waiting for me when I returned to our station. I recognized that certain look I had seen a dozen times. I was in for a lecture. "Sit down, Phillip," he began, using my full name for the first time. Very deliberately, Sam lit a cigarette and continued. "This is the last push—then it's over." With his chin pressed firmly in his chest, his bug-eyes stared at me to emphasize the weight of his statement.

"Yeah, I know," I said with a blank expression.

"Do you?"

"Could it be any worse than the Fourth of July?"

"Maybe not in numbers." Sam shook his head slowly side to side. "But it will be the last time. No more polishing silverware for you. No more fetching prune juice. No more listening to an alta cocker waiter...."

Only then did I realize what Sam was talking about. It had nothing to do with the big week-end. I had been so wrapped up with Laurie and then not having her that it didn't occur to me that my special connection to Sam might be running its course. Aside from Laurie, Sam was one of the few people around that I really cared about. Sam was trying to tell me, without saying so, that he was going to miss *me*. Embarrassed, yet touched, I chirped, "Hey, this summer was practice. Next year we're gonna knock 'em dead."

"You're coming back?"

"I need the money, money, money, money. Besides,...I like working with you, Sam."

"What! By next summer, you'll be a waiter yourself."

"Actually, Sam," my enthusiasm now dwindled to a mutter, "I don't think Diana wants me back. She's kind of pissed off at me."

"Why? You're a good worker. I tell her all the time."

"It has nothing to do with work," I said glumly.

"Ah,...." Sam whispered, raising his head, eyes popping. "It's about the important things."

Being spared the reminder that I was warned early in the summer about Joann, I responded nonetheless. "I know, I know all about it. But it's not that easy."

"Don't worry, boychik. Let's take one thing at a time. So you don't win the Ass-Kisser's award this year. Big deal. I've learned that you can't plan too much into the future. God doesn't like that. He wants to see humility and a little more respect for the big picture. So, in the meantime, let's look at tonight's menu and do the best we can with it."

Shabbat dinner. Always the same—but this time, the same for the last time. A slab of gefilte fish on a piece of lettuce, topped with a slice of carrot and a dash of deep red horse radish, designed to clean the sinuses and all other passages. Matzoh ball soup—always too hot and, as Sam always notes, never lies still in the bowl. From there it starts to vary. The more flanken orders, the more elderly folks in the food pool. Mixed feelings for me as I went through the last go-around of a ritual. Good riddance and a sadness at the same time. My heart was already in the big city.

Saturday blurred into Sunday. Labor Day arrived almost anti-climactically, sneaking in on the wake of a cloudy sunrise. The morning passed without event. Then Mr. Arthur called a meeting.

"Thank God it's the last day," Bobby Meyers sighed. "I swear, we have more meetings than General Motors."

"Quiet," shushed Stan. "It's time for the Kiss My Ass award."

"Okay, gentlemen," the maitre d' began with uncharacteristic good cheer. Even the brass buttons on his blue blazer seemed to take on a special sheen. "As you know, the lunch meal will be the last one for all of you except Sam. I'm sure you'll be anxious to hit the road as soon as possible so I'll just make a few remarks now....... Any comments from you boys before I start?"

Murray stood up and shuffled a bit. "All in all, I think it was a pretty good summer," he started, looking around at his peers. "And on behalf of the staff, I'd like to thank you for your understanding and for putting up with us."

"Well, thank you, Koenig. I really appreciate that," a behumbled Mr. Arthur responded.

Danny turned and mumbled, "Isn't it a little late for brown-nosing?" The others giggled but Mr. Arthur ignored the exchange and continued.

"Yes, it has been a decent season. With a few exceptions, the Millers and I have been satisfied with your performances."

"Always qualifying," Stan whispered to me. "Why can't the prick say something nice and just leave it?" He rocked uneasily on the back legs of his chair.

"Before you leave the dining room, there will be an accounting of all silverware and you will leave your stations spotless. I will check personally." Mr. Arthur then extracted an envelope from his vest pocket and recited, "For those of you new this summer, it has become customary the past few years for Mrs. Miller to present the Karl Miller Award at this time. It's a monetary stipend of fifty dollars in the name of her late father-in-law, Karl Miller. Unfortunately, she is unable to be with us this morning, so on her behalf I will make the presentation. The award is meant to reward the member of the dining room staff who best exemplifies the spirit of service, cooperation and hospitality, so much a part of the Miller philosophy of running a hotel. This year the award goes to......Sidney Goldhammer."

Hoots and whistles rang out as the red-faced law student accepted the envelope. "Now you can take us all out for a beer, moneybags!" Myron shouted.

"For once, they did something right," Stan mumbled.

\* \* \*

The last meal came and went. The staff hastily went about its last clean-up mission, intermittently stealing a moment to count last-minute tips. A mixed feeling of euphoria and sadness pervaded the room as Bobby

Meyers could be heard chanting, "No more fucking goblets. No more polishing fucking silverware. No more setting fucking tables...."

Mr. Arthur entered and started making his rounds, inspecting each station with the intensity of a Marine sergeant, just short of administering the white glove treatment. When Sam and I finally passed muster, we saluted him, bowed to each other, then embraced in a silent, warm hug. We knew this was good-bye.

By three o'clock most of the staff had evacuated the hotel, assembling in the rear parking lot to say our last farewells. Waving his camera wildly, Danny tried to choreograph group pictures, preferably featuring an up-turned middle-finger, or at least a cross-eyed grimace. Myron Smith accommodated with both, sitting on Sid's lap, front and center. Then the scramble began, with five guys trying to squeeze themselves and a summer's worth of gear into two small cars for the ride home. Murray's was the first to leave. With suitcases tied precariously to its roof, the white VW bug churned off onto the gravel driveway. Just before it turned the corner, Myron leaned way out of the rear window with outstretched arms and yelled, "Hey guys, I didn't win any Ass-Kissing award, but look what I've got!" He playfully dangled a little tin bell, then proceeded to ring it wildly, laughing crazily as the car disappeared into the dust. It was, of course, Mr. Arthur's.

# CHAPTER 28

Crossing the George Washington Bridge was always a welcome homecoming for me. And it was the panoramic view of Manhattan from this perspective that made me glad, even proud to live in New York. At the extreme right of the staggered stone horizon called downtown, the Empire State Building, along with its lesser known cousins, reached up to penetrate the hazy sky. To the left, capped with the mighty spectre of the Cloisters, the terraced oasis of green called Fort Tryon Park rose elegantly from its base at the Hudson River. And straight ahead, the five stately towers of the Castle Village apartments heralded the entrance to Washington Heights.

Stan Simon left the motor running as he tossed my duffle bag to the sidewalk. We looked at each other and nodded in silent agreement; the summer had been a good one. "Well, buddy, that's it," Stan said. "Your momma can't complain that I didn't deliver you safe and sound."

"Yeah, that was great." I just couldn't bring myself to say thanks. We had done too much together.

"We're gonna get together, right?" Stan pushed.

"Yeah, sure," I confirmed. "I'll give you a call as soon as I'm settled at school."

"Don't bullshit me, now."

"Hey, would I do that to you, the horny sex-fiend who stranded me in the god-damned Garlands parking lot?"

"Shit, you'll never let me live that down."

"Never," I answered with a big smile. The two of us stood on the sidewalk between the durable Simobile and my meager luggage and just looked around, waiting for a way to say goodbye.

"Well, I gotta go," he said. "I'm low on gas and wouldn't want to run out in this god-forsaken part of the city."

"Yeah, you're right," I agreed. "Go home to that rat-hole called Brooklyn and run out there." I picked up my bags and watched Stan drive off. The hug we both felt never came.

I started walking to my apartment building, feeling like a returning warrior, having just completed his first tour of duty as a mountain rat. Inhaling the neighborhood air, I sensed that certain nostalgic post-Labor Day humidity that only existed in New York City. I was home again.

So much had happened in the last three months, yet the building's front door squeaked exactly as it always had—and the elevator button dinged the same as it had the previous May. Comforting to me, but at the same time I felt sorry for these poor inanimate objects, deprived of the precious experience of feeling and change. I smiled as the familiar stale smell of the elevator cab hit me, remembering how as a five-year-old I would wedge myself in a corner with legs spread, bracing myself for an imagined free-fall through the elevator shaft.

Putting my bags down in front of my apartment door, I hesitated before ringing the doorbell. I hoped my father would be home. I might get some breathing space—not be pounced upon by my mother and grilled about every detail of the summer. Luckily, Fred Dechter answered the door. Looking tired and slightly hunched in his pale blue cardigan sweater, he welcomed me with a silent smile.

"Hi, Pop. It's your long lost son."

"I see that," the elder Dechter said with eyes twinkling. "Put your things down and give me a hug. You look older. It must have been a long summer."

"You look great," I lied as I embraced my father. "I thought you and Mom were going to visit me. You must have been having too good a time at your swim club."

"Oh, the club is alright. I just couldn't get away from the office. I'm sorry."

"It's okay, Pop." I knew my father's desk job did not carry the responsibility he would have liked and was extremely sensitive to any slight to his imagined status. It had not always been that way in Vienna where the name Friedrich Dechter had carried real weight in business circles. But the world had changed dramatically in the last twenty years and he had gotten off with a relatively light sentence from the rampages of Hitler. Yes, he was still alive, but was never able to pick up in this country where he dropped off in the old.

My mother made a dinner fit for a returning prince—but it had its price. I was expected to recount each day of the summer, complete with meals, names of big tippers, and descriptions of my bosses and co-workers. I was careful to tread lightly around my love life, but did hint that I might have met someone. When pressed by my mother to elaborate, I suddenly and conveniently remembered Lisa's visit. "She came out of nowhere," I began, "and surprised the heck out of me. It was great. Boy, did she impress my waiter."

"Lisa can be very impressive when she wants to be," her father said proudly.

"I know. She seems to have made quite an impression on her stage manager, too. I met him when I went to see her play."

"We know all about it," mom said slyly.

"About Mitch Gustafson?"

"About him and also about your visit with a special friend." She made no secret of her pleasure in having her son aware of her omniscience.

"What do you think of Lisa going out with a non-Jew?" I asked quickly.

"It happens. We're not crazy about it, but it happens," my father said wearily. "She's already changed her name."

"What if she marries the guy? What about children?"

"Don't worry so much. You sound like a grandmother," my mother said, shrugging off my concern as she started to clear the table. "Lisa isn't thinking about marriage right now. God willing, she has a career and she's giving everything she has to it. Bless her."

I stared at the ceiling and sighed, "Sure would be nice if she met the right guy. It would be neat to be an uncle."

"There's much time for all that. Why don't the two of you go out for a nice walk while I do the dishes. The air is so nice." She looked at me a long time then squeezed my cheeks with both hands and kissed my forehead. "It's nice to have my little boy home again." I winced privately, but accepted her affection and even returned the kiss.

* * *

The evening air picked up the breeze coming up off the Hudson as father and son strolled down Cabrini Boulevard toward Fort Tryon Park. I was the taller of the two of us by three inches, yet our gait was in unison. At first we walked in silence, enjoying each other's presence and the surroundings we knew so well. This ritual had become scarcer since I entered college, and for that reason, more precious.

We passed the last stretch of six story brick apartment buildings. I gazed down the steeply embanked wooded area separating the sidewalk from the river, several hundred feet below. As a child, I had called this area "the wilderness," where my father and I would discover new trails and secret hiding places during our Sunday morning romps. Now, as we walked, I wondered if our adventures had been an escape for my father as well.

"You know, Pop, of all the refugees I met this summer none were from Vienna...... Too bad," I added

"Why? What difference does it make?"

"Oh—every once in a while—and especially this past summer, I try to imagine what would have been if we didn't have to leave."

"Ha!" my father laughed without smiling. "I think about it every day."

Without breaking stride, I was shocked to hear this coming from the man who had only spoken of fleeing Austria as little more than an unfortunate inconvenience. "I mean, aside from just barely being born there, whatever I know of Vienna I've learned from you and Mom—which wasn't much. If Hitler had never come, we'd still be there. I'd probably be sitting at a sidewalk cafe right now drinking coffee with *schlogobers*." We paused and leaned on the railing to watch the sun slowly set behind the Palisades.

"Isn't the bridge beautiful—now with the lights?" Fred Dechter pondered, not following his son's line of thought. "Look at all the cars coming back from the summer. There's a story inside each one."

"Pop!" I interjected, almost shouting with frustration. "I'm trying to figure out *our* story!"

He looked at me calmly. "Our story was interrupted. We're doing the best we can."

"I know all that. We're not a regular American family no matter what we do. I wish I knew who we really were."

"What we were, we cannot be. When circumstances change, we must change with them—or we are lost." The overhead streetlight glared down on my father at a strange angle, giving him an eerie glow of urgency.

"I guess, but I think someday I'd really like to go to Vienna—walk the streets, see the buildings, smell the air that I would have smelled."

"Don't get too romantic with your ideas of the city of waltzes. I have wonderful memories that were real. But the last memories are the ones that stick. When the people you consider your friends turn their backs on you, when your business partners promise you protection and can't deliver—it leaves a bitter taste—that is if you can survive to taste anything at all. Everything boils down to people and character. No, *I* have no desire, myself, to go back."

# CHAPTER 29

The number "4" bus groaned down Fort Washington Avenue, then made the lazy turn onto Broadway just as it had every day during my commute to Columbia the previous year. The trip itself took only about twenty five minutes but seemed endless, screeching from stop to stop along the stretch of Hispanic fruit stores before reaching the express run to Riverside Drive. I hated the boring drone of it all and had thought of living at the TAP House my sophomore year, but never got around to pursuing the money angle. My parents would have thought it a frivolous and unnecessary expense. I got off at 114th Street and started walking up the steeply inclined sidewalk.

The three-story limestone townhouse known as Tau Alpha Pi looked out of place, squeezed in among the tall drab brick buildings surrounding it. Usually the noisiest structure on the block, it appeared somber on this gray Wednesday morning after the Labor Day week-end. I took the entry steps three at a time, anxious to find life within, particularly among my sophomore peers. I heard laughter coming from the kitchen and found Josh Spiegelman and Herbie Altschuler chomping on donuts while listening to Bruce Klein relate his summer adventures. Seeing me, Bruce interrupted his story and called out, "Hey, it's the return of the Ass-man mountain rat! How'd the summer go?"

"Great! Great! How are you guys?"

"Did you get laid?" Josh Spiegelman asked without fanfare.

"None of your fucking business," I answered, irritated.

"Is that a 'yes' or a 'no'?" Herbie inquired, his eyebrows arching over his horn-rimmed glasses.

Bruce Klein tried to help out. "It's either a reluctant 'no' or a 'yes' that you're not supposed to know about."

I shook my head. "You guys are pathetic.... Are there any donuts left?" The other three looked at each other with quizzical interest.

Herbie Altschuler finally said, "That's not a very brotherly response. You're supposed to share your innermost thoughts with us. Remember us? We're your confidants, the guys you pledged this house with."

"Okay, you clowns win. You really want my innermost thoughts? I really, really, really.... want a donut, preferably double chocolate."

"Hey, the guy sounds serious," Bruce said thoughtfully, his acne still intact. "Don't tell me you pined away for Carol all summer long."

"Carol," I repeated with surprise, trying to put her in context. "No. Actually I met somebody new, someone very special."

"Aha!" Josh exclaimed. "Now we're getting somewhere. Give him a donut. Maybe he'll tell us more."

With a mouthful of French Cruller, the last donut in the box, I said, "She's great. Her name's Laurie and......I'll bring her around. You'll see." I was already sorry I said anything. I felt almost immediately when I mentioned her name that I had cheapened Laurie's image........ And the donut wasn't even chocolate.

\* \* \*

Tweed herringbone got thicker on campus as the week progressed. So did the sight of pale blue beanies atop incoming freshmen. "We're not the bottom of the heap anymore, Brucey," I observed with a hint of superiority, as he and I perused the bookstore for our new semester's texts.

"Yeah," Bruce Klein said dreamily. "Now if we could only channel our new status into working for us. You think we should clamp down on new pledges like those assholes did to us?"

"I don't think I could do that. It becomes a vicious cycle. I know there's supposed to be a method to the madness, but I still have a bad taste from last year,......so, at least for myself, I don't think I've got it in me to harass anyone at this point."

"Don't get philosophical on me. I just want to know how to use this new power," Bruce laughed. "Let's go to the West End for a beer and talk about it."

Walking down Broadway, I tried to imagine Laurie next to me, not my pimpled, albeit amusing fraternity brother. How I would strut with her—and when cooler weather came, I would get her one of those long, baby blue and white Columbia scarves. Not only would it keep her warm, but identify her as mine when she's out of range. I had difficulty picturing her face—not the first time, but it upset me nevertheless. I gazed at the few passing Barnard co-eds, but found not a trace of Laurie's spark within them. They all had bland, almost non-existent eyebrows. What I did notice was a distinct smell to the neighborhood, one I remembered from the previous year. It was a combination of bus exhaust, Chock Full O' Nuts coffee and rancid river air coming up from the Hudson. As a definer of locale, I liked it. "I hear you're going to live at the House this year," I said to Bruce.

"Yeah, coming in from Queens was a real drag last year. You're lucky you live so close."

"I don't know about lucky. I just can't justify living on campus while having a free bed waiting for me in Washington Heights. But it would be great being around here."

"Yeah, if you and me were roomies, we'd have parties every night. Say, when am I going to meet your doll? Is she real?" he asked.

"I haven't seen her myself since camp ended. Hunter doesn't start till late September so her parents planned a little family trip to the Berkshires. I really miss her."

"Any pictures?" Bruce asked.

"No pictures. By the way, I never asked you if you were still seeing that girl Myrna?"

"Yeah. Actually I've seen a lot of her this summer. I'm thinking of giving her my pin this fall."

I stopped walking and stared at my friend. "Your pin! That's serious stuff. Isn't it a little early for that?"

\* \* \*

Laurie would be home by Sunday afternoon. I waited till evening when my parents were at a movie before attempting to call. I sat by the phone and tried to picture her. Again her image escaped me. It had been too long a time since I saw her and the prospect of speaking to her both excited and scared me. What to say? Had her feelings changed? I stared at the instrument. When I finally dialed her number, my palms were wet.

A snickering teen-aged male voice answered, "Stillman residence." After asking for Laurie, I was put on hold for what seemed like a very long time. Finally, the kid returned, telling me Laurie would call back in half an hour. I sat in the dark wondering whether something was wrong. While I hadn't even heard her voice, the whole transaction just didn't sound right. Was her home life different from the sweetness and light I had imagined? I would just have to wait and see. Fifty minutes later, Laurie called.

"I have to see you," she said bluntly.

"Is that a hello?" I asked, puzzled.

"Sorry, I can't talk long. But I have to see you," she repeated nervously.

"Is anything wrong?"

"Where can we meet?"

"Anywhere. You name it," I chuckled apprehensively. "I missed you. How about on campus?"

"No! Not there..... Central Park......tomorrow afternoon." There was no joy in her voice.

"Sure, where?"

"Columbus Circle at 2 o'clock."

"Fine."

"I can't talk. Goodbye."

By the time I said goodbye, I was talking to a dial tone. I remained by the phone for a long time, then went to the bathroom and looked in the mirror. I saw a pale, scared young man wondering what had gone wrong.

* * *

The subway ride was long. The few people who shared the car with me were oblivious to my anxiety. One elderly woman snored as she dozed open-mouthed, sitting with her shopping bags secured tightly between her legs. A younger man hanging on an overhead strap, hovered over her, reading a foreign language newspaper. I stared out the blackened window, waiting for the 59th Street station to appear. I hadn't seen Laurie in almost three weeks and had hoped our reunion would be a romantic one. Maybe it still could be.

Darting up the stairs to the street level, the smell and the sounds of the city returned. A strange mixture of retirees and young women with baby carriages lined the benches guarding the entrance points to the park. I searched for signs of Laurie but only found huddling strangers, scurrying businessmen and children feeding pigeons. Would she be coming from the bustling traffic of the Circle or emerge from the tranquility of Central Park itself? Then I saw her, only because she was such a solitary figure, standing small and motionless in front of the huge stone entrance gate.

Running over, I greeted her with a soft kiss. Almost instantly, the gesture felt perfunctory. She looked at me intently, her eyebrows knit with purpose, then took my hand and said simply, "Let's walk."

As we strode into the park without a word, I thought she looked tired. Her gaze was fixed on the pavement. When the silence got too overbearing for me, I tried to make light of my feeling. "You really scared me on the phone. Has your brother been getting on your nerves or something?"

"No..... Let's sit down." Laurie led me off the path toward a large rock formation in the middle of a meadow. Nearby, young children were happily playing on monkey bars and swings. With the two of us strolling hand in hand and a bright cloudless sky overhead, the scene must have looked idyllic, everything I had envisioned the reunion would be—but my instincts told me different. Once settled on the rock, Laurie again peered at me, and with great difficulty mouthed the words, "Something *is* wrong."

"I can see that," I said softly.

Her eyes welling with tears, she whispered, "Something happened that shouldn't have happened." I was puzzled and remained quiet, but my heart beat wildly. I waited.

"I'm pregnant!" she blurted. Only then did the tears flow.

I froze. I could not talk. I could not breath. I could not console her. A dizziness came over me as I stared at Laurie who was now crying uncontrollably, her head buried between her folded knees.

"You sure?" he finally asked, weakly.

"Yes, I'm sure," she yelled.

"You mean that night across the lake?"

"When else?" Her nose started to run.

Still dazed, I continued to stare as she sobbed. The world around me ceased to move. Visions of medical school came to me and suddenly the prospect seemed beyond reach. "How could she do this to me?" I

GEORGE ERDSTEIN

thought. Everything had been set. I would work hard through high school to get into a good college. I would then work hard in college to get into a medical school. Somewhere along the line I would meet a beautiful and supportive girl who I would marry when the time was right. This is what Jewish boys did. This is what they had to do. "Who else knows?" I asked.

"No one. Do you know how hard it's been keeping this to myself? I'm so ashamed." She leaned toward me, wanting to be cradled.

"I'm trying to think," I said stiffly, defending my lack of response. "We've got to do something. We're not ready for this."

Laurie's tears dried as her eyes widened. "You want me to have an abortion, don't you?"

"Don't *you?*"

"I don't know. That's why we're talking. I just can't face my parents with it. And I don't know who else to talk to." She started sobbing again.

"I don't know how these things work but don't we have a little time?"

"Not much. I'm so confused."

"I know a couple of guys I'd like to talk to. They know about these things."

"I don't want any back alley butcher working on me," Laurie insisted.

I finally reached out to her and held her tight. "Don't worry. I won't let that happen. It'll be safe. I promise." I closed my eyes and hoped.

With hands clasped, we walked back to Columbus Circle in silence. Unfairly, the sky was even bluer than before. I looked at Laurie and kissed her closed eyelids, then her eyebrows. "Don't tell anyone yet," I whispered. "I'll call you in a couple of days when I know something." Then we parted.

190

# CHAPTER 30

"Shit! Shit! Shit!" I banged my head softly against the dark subway window. What had I gotten myself into? Earlier that morning I had asked Buddy Marks, my all-knowing senior fraternity brother, where a neighborhood friend of mine might seek help after getting a girl "in trouble." Surprisingly, Buddy was quite helpful. Because I was his "Little Brother" in good standing, he immediately made a phone call to a family acquaintance who had been a surgeon in Germany. Unable to secure a license to practice in the United States, according to Buddy, this man did consultancy on a limited basis on matters of this sort and still considered himself a physician.

Because of the sensitive nature of my inquiry, I was, on my friend's behalf, to meet discreetly with the good doctor that afternoon, without further questions. So instead of preparing for my new fall classes, I was on my way to rendezvous with the mysterious Dr. Ehrlich. "Probably not his real name," I thought as I approached the dingy brownstone on West 74th Street. If Buddy hadn't already set up the appointment, I, too, would have used a false name. But here I was, climbing three flights of musty stairs leading to either freedom or further doom.

I rang the bell to what was not even an office, but an apartment. The tiny label beneath the peephole did, however, read, "Dr. Claus Ehrlich."

A small, bald, bony man wearing rimless glasses, bow tie, and shabby vested suit, came to the door. Gesturing a broad welcome belying his frail stature, he led me into a tight, dimly lit study. While the room was totally devoid of color, I was somewhat becalmed by the impressive array of framed certificates gracing one wall. The little man pointed to a black leather lounge chair, so crackled with age as to resemble a map of intricate rivers and tributaries. As I sat down, I wondered how many would-be fathers had squirmed in its comfort before me. Dr. Ehrlich took a seat behind his desk, folded his hands, and studied his visitor through blurry bifocals. "You must be a very good friend," he began in a deliberate, slightly Teutonic tone.

I nodded in confirmation.

"What shall I call your friend?"

"His name is Greg Easton," I said without hesitation, satisfied that I could finally use the name I had saved all my life—not for a situation like this, but for when, in my fantasy, I would need an alter-ego to fend off a would-be kidnapper or the like.

"And *his* good friend?"

"Sandy."

Clasping his hands behind his head and leaning back, Dr. Ehrlich stared at the ceiling. "Tell me a little about the relationship between Greg Easton and his friend Sandy."

Impatient, I blurted, "They need an abortion!"

"No, no, no. We don't talk like that." Dr, Ehrlich waved his finger sideways in admonition. "Don't you know that it is illegal to perform an abortion? We are here to discuss your friend's situation. If it turns out that there is a gynecological problem, there are procedures that can be administered to remedy the problem. But we are not there yet. Now, I ask you again to tell me about the couple. Are they in love, or....," fluttering his hands, "was this what you call a 'one night stand'?"

I didn't understand why this man was asking these questions but somehow, through all the hyperbole and cloak and dagger tactics, I trusted him. "I think they're very much in love," I said slowly. "They just made a mistake. It was just the wrong time...... It was definitely not a one night stand." I fidgeted in my chair, then continued. "He wanted everything to go just right. This was meant to be.... long range. Now it's all ruined....unless they have a.... *procedure*."

"And that would solve everything?"

"Yeah...... It would have to be safe, of course," I added with a self-righteous nod.

Dr. Ehrlich leaned forward. "First let me tell you something. "*They* don't have a procedure. *The girl* goes through the procedure. God-willing, it is successful. I have done many, many of these—all successful, but there are no guarantees. Her partner, meanwhile, waits outside and hopes it all goes away. He will be free. Perhaps not from guilt, but free nevertheless." His magnified eyes pierced mine as he continued. "There is a name for the procedure. It is Dilation and Curettage, an acceptable practice that usually, as a side effect, does away with any fetus present. It is also known as a D & C, and sometimes referred to euphemistically, in the trade, as 'dusting and cleaning'." I chuckled nervously. "But it is never called an abortion." Again he glared at his visitor. "You used the phrase, 'all ruined.' Just what is all ruined?"

"His career," I shrugged, as if it were obvious.

The little man got out of his chair and started pacing the small available floor space, his hands now clasped firmly behind his back. "His career," he repeated in deep deliberation. My thoughts drifted to a typical sunny Sunday afternoon when throngs of former Europeans would stroll the main promenade of Fort Tryon Park, the women parading their finest furs while the men debated, their stance and gait not unlike that of Dr. Ehrlich, patrolling his turf in his own miniscule domain. "Tell me," his surprisingly robust voice boomed at me, "do you think that everything in life is a straight line from *A* to *Z*?"

"What do you mean?"

"Sometimes there are little bends and diversions in the road. It could be a failed grade, a death in the family, a plunge in the stock market, or a holocaust intended to wipe out an entire people—something that takes you off your intended path. With cunning and luck—and some think also with a little help from a higher power, there's a chance one can get back on course—or you can end up in the wilderness. It's all part of life. You're young. You probably haven't seen too many bumps yet. Yes, this is definitely a bump in the road—and there are choices to be made."

Waiting for a reaction from me but finding none, he sat down and continued. "Before there is a decision, let me tell you a little story—a true story. A long time ago when I was a medical student in Berlin, I too had dear friends. Only they were married and very much in love. They had everything to look forward to. As it happened, the young and lovely bride got pregnant, something the young couple had not yet planned for. They wanted to do a little 'living' before settling down. Traveling, skiing, who knows. And abortion was not the taboo it is in this country. In short, it was not *convenient* for this young couple to have a child at the time. Oh, they loved children and looked forward to having them, but only when the time was right. So they merrily went ahead with an abortion. But something happened. No, she didn't die. The operation was successful—too successful. She was unable to conceive again.....And so, because they wanted to extend their playful youth a little longer, they had to live with that decision the rest of their lives."

Waiting for the story to register, Ehrlich tapped his fingertips together, then looked sternly into my eyes. "If you choose to proceed,....or I should say, if your friend and his partner choose to go ahead—this is the arrangement. If, after a preliminary examination of the young lady, I find she is no more than six weeks pregnant but otherwise healthy, I will expect $200 in cash." He smiled oddly as he added, "Insurance policies don't count in my office. Another $200 is to be paid at the end of the procedure." Standing abruptly, Dr. Ehrlich extended his hand and said, "Good day. Give my best to the young lady."

More confused than before, I left the building and started wandering in a southward direction. Turning on 72nd Street, I passed the Eclair Coffee Shop, famed refuge for displaced Europeans longing for earlier times and another creme-filled *Napoleon*. Even on a weekday afternoon, the sidewalk tables were filled with aging coffee-drinkers enjoying their traditional *jause*. They seemed oblivious to the mundane traffic surrounding them, concentrating rather on the ashes of their extended cigarettes and a far-away world of leisure in three-quarter time. I inhaled the aroma of New York's finest pastries but knew this was no time to indulge myself. I quickened my pace, not quite sure where I was going. Forced to stop by a red traffic light at the next corner, I felt beads of sweat forming on my forehead and upper lip. My heart was thumping relentlessly. This was no place to think and I desperately had to think. Poor Laurie. She had left this in my hands and I didn't know if I was up to it. There was no let up to the pounding in my chest. I had to get away. Somewhere to think. Somewhere quiet.

\* \* \*

The next morning I took the family car. Telling my father I had to help a friend move into the fraternity house, I headed east on the Cross-Bronx Expressway toward the Long Island beaches. The day was gray and blustery. Strong winds bucked the car's progress as if to say, "Don't run away. Stay and face the music." But the need to be at Jones Beach got stronger with each mile, perhaps *because* of the weather. Soon I was the only driver on the road.

The beach had never been a great summer attraction for me. Climbing over a multitude of prone bodies on scorchingly hot sand just to get to salty water one couldn't even swim in was not my idea of a good time. And getting clammy sand particles out of the deep crevices of one's body was not among my favorite childhood memories. But the beach in off-season was something totally different. It could be a wonderfully lonely place, open to imagination and full of mystery. In winter months, it represented raw nature at its beguiling best. And now, for me, it offered solitude.

Swirls of loose flying sand attacked the windshield as I pulled into the desolate parking lot. Slamming the car door, I turned up my collar and fought my way into the wind toward that endless but ever-changing line where beach meets water. Acknowledged only by a few stray gulls, I took off my shoes and let my feet sink into the cool, soothing clay-like sand. Forming a trail of deep footprints, I approached the ocean. Beneath the cold silver sky, dark ominous waves thrashed toward the shoreline, dissipating meekly as they surrendered at my welcoming ankles. I searched the white sands for something to return to the sea, but the few fragments of shells I found would not do. This was not a venue for skipping stones. It had a higher purpose.

Perching myself on a driftwood log, I scanned the vast horizon. Off in the distance, what appeared to be two figures, were approaching from the south. They moved gracefully, despite walking directly into the wind. The taller, a man, had his arm around his diminutive partner, guiding her through the sand. Dressed in dark business clothes, the pair looked odd yet familiar to me. I could not place them. As they passed, I could see their pained expressions. If they were struggling, why were they here? Where were they going? Then I recognized them. It was Marcel and Tina Hauser. They looked so utterly forlorn. I called to them, but they did not hear. Soon they were gone and I was alone again.

As high tide rolled in, waves began to lick at my uneasy throne. Reluctantly, I got up and started working my way southward with the wind at my back, all the while trying to concentrate on what might be the decision of my life—a decision with a time clock—one which could not be put off. To have the abortion, assumed safe, would almost surely end my relationship with Laurie, but keep me, sort of, on track. Not to have the abortion—I couldn't begin to contemplate it. Suddenly I heard laughter. I turned to see two men squatting in the sand with a game board between them. Around them, a young girl was dancing, her long pink dress held above her naked ankles by her dainty fingers. She continued to laugh as the men engaged in their heated play. Upon closer inspection, I found that the game was chess and the participants were Dr. Ehrlich and Sam Schectman, my beloved waiter. I greeted them but they were too steeped in concentration to pay me any attention. Observing their moves, I was soon confused by their seeming disregard for the safety of the higher officers. Priding myself as a better than average player, I finally blurted out in frustration, "Sam, what did you do that for?"

Sam waved me off impatiently, saying, "Boychik, just watch..... When Ehrlich and I play, the rules change. The pawns are what count. They're the future. It's the young pawns we must protect, not the old king."

"Quiet," an insistent Dr. Ehrlich interrupted. "I'm trying to think." The wind worked swirls of sand around the players, causing Sam's thinning hair to dance wildly. He looked comfortable in his open white-on-white shirt, while Dr. Ehrlich's severe dark tie fluttered nervously in the breeze.

I sat down to watch the game more closely. Ehrlich turned to me and said, "I'll be in my office later this afternoon. I'm still waiting for your response." Soon there were only pawns left on the board—Sam's five to Ehrlich's two. The good doctor sighed deeply, "Okay, Schechtman, I concede. This time, you win."

A twinkle appeared in Sam's eye as he addressed me. "You see, my friend, you don't always have to have a diploma on the wall to win in this game. You just have to know the right thing to do." Then getting up, he cupped his hands to light a cigarette and inhaled with great satisfaction. Without another word, he strode off along the beach with Shana close behind, dancing and giggling until they both disappeared into the horizon. So intently did my gaze follow them, I did not notice that Dr. Ehrlich, too, had vanished, leaving no trace of either the game or his imprint in the sand.

Again, I was alone. But somehow it was not the same. Something was different. Something had changed. Something was stirring inside me. I stood up and faced the ocean. As the waves rushed toward me, I raised my arms to catch the full brunt of the wind coming in, closing my eyes to let the salty mist flush my face. The pounding of my heart reinforced the urgency of the moment. Suddenly I knew what to do. I started to walk, then jog away from the beach. Soon I was running at full speed toward the parking lot. "He's right," I screamed. "It's about life!"

# EPILOGUE

I took off my sunglasses as the unpredictable Michigan sky started to turn gray. Having just passed through a four mile construction zone restricting traffic to a single lane, I felt strained and longed for relief. I heard rustling, followed by a loud, unrestrained yawn coming from the back of the van. I asked, "Is that you, Marc?"

"Yup!" a deep, tired voice responded.

"How about giving your old man a break and taking over at the wheel?"

"Dad, I need all the rest I can get," the voice objected.

"All you did was rest for the last two weeks."

"Dad, I'm saving my energy. I'm twenty two years old. You know how it is. I'm starting medical school in three days. You told me yourself they're gonna run me ragged and I'm not going to sleep until I graduate."

"Don't exaggerate. I'm pulling over at the next rest stop." I then glanced into the rear-view mirror, catching my son stretch his long arms and rub his dark, bushy eyebrows. Soon another occupant came to life.

"Oh, Phil, why don't you lighten up?" my wife offered. "Marc needs his sleep."

Immediately, a young girl's voice piped up from under a blanket, protesting, "Mom's always defending Marc."

The subject of conversation beamed a broad smile and laughed, "That's 'cause she gets her good looks from me."

The road soon opened to its full three lanes—smooth, but ever-winding. And the van followed.

Breinigsville, PA USA
16 December 2009
229361BV00001B/103/A